MY BELOVED BORINQUEN

◀ A NOVEL ▶

JOHN DAVID FERRER

Cover Art by Robert Thibeault

Photographs by the Puerto Rico Historic Buildings Drawings Society

Interior design by Dave Pasquantonio

ISBN 979-8-218-13386-3 (print)

Published by John David Publishing, Framingham, MA

This novel is dedicated to a lifelong friend, Rafael Cortes, who served as my beta reader in four novels, acted as a Spanish language proofreader, and more importantly, is one of the most outstanding human beings I have ever had as a close friend.

.

Contents

Part One

Chapter 1
Escape From The Republic

G abriela Penélope Díaz hadn't slept for days. The continued
bombing at night of Barcelona in the last days of the Spanish
Civil War made sleep impossible. The Fascists were closing in on the
city. The German bombers, which included Savoia 81 aircraft and
parts of the Condor Legion of the Luftwaffe, strafed the streets of
Barcelona and the *Barrio Gòtico* mercilessly. They would start the
attack at 12:30 a.m. and continue until the wee hours of the morning.
Anyone caught in the deluge of steel and machine gun bullets, be it a
woman, a child, or the elderly, didn't stand a chance. Bodies were
littered everywhere for days. It was an existence of fire, bomb blasts,
missing limbs, destruction, and sheer terror. The *barrio* had been
ravaged—old storefronts burned, alleyways which were once romantic
paths now filled with debris and remnants of rooftops which had
survived for hundreds of years.

Gabriela awoke that morning of January 1939 with the conviction
that she and her family had to leave Spain. The Loyalist Republicans
were losing the war. And it was just a matter of time before the Nationalists, led by General Franco, vanquished them. Then Nationalists

would start their vengeance. This would include executions, persecutions, rapes, imprisonments, and more. She had to save herself and her family. The Republican government had announced that in the next compulsory draft for military service, the minimum age would be lowered to 16. Her only son, Fernando, was 14.

Their residence was on the Carrer Escudelles, not far from the Ayuntamiento, the central municipal offices, the latter a frequent target of the aircraft. While their old stucco house was of sturdy construction, and had two floors with a small cellar, it wasn't strong enough to protect her family from the shock waves caused by the bombs and falling debris. Parts of the outer walls were beginning to crack, and the family refuge, the cellar, was dark, damp, and smelled of urine. It barely had room for Fernando and her daughter, Teresa.

The children reacted differently to the crises. Fernando, scrawny and thin, was withdrawn, sullen, and hardly spoke a word. Teresa, a delicate creature, would wince and start crying when she heard the frequent gunfire and multiple explosions.

Gabriela had moved out of her former grandparents' house in the Eixample, the Casa Roche, soon after she was married to Carmelo Díaz, a strong supporter of the Republican cause who had volunteered to fight the army rebellion. She had met him at a society ball years ago and had fallen for him that same night. Bored by the same status-seeking gentlemen who courted her, she found Carmelo different, from a well-to-do family but not enamored of Barcelona high society. Dark skinned like the Andalusians, with chestnut colored hair and long sideburns, he had an air of grace, courage, and dignity.

Her parents had been aghast at her choice since they were very conservative and dedicated monarchists. They had all but forbidden the marriage. Gabriela had prevailed. She had a way with her mother, Penélope, and was able to convince her that Carmelo was the man she truly loved. Her grandfather, Agustin Roche, who died from tuberculosis shortly after her marriage, remained opposed to the union until his death, in the same manner he had rejected his own son, Antonio, and his rebellious politics. Gabriela had heard stories from her mother about Antonio's fortunes in Puerto Rico—the people, the beauty of the island, and that she had considered moving there someday.

The years had passed, but they had been kind to Gabriela. She wore her naturally straight silky black hair in long tresses; they had not yet streaked gray. Her wrinkles, at 39 years, were barely noticeable. Gabriela Díaz had been the belle of the ball in her adolescence, one of the most attractive young women in Barcelona circles. She was her mother's spitting image, and her laughter, in better times, had been infectious, just like her mother's.

Now, as head of the household, she had to make plans for a departure from Spain. Carmelo, her husband, had been killed by enemy aircraft machine guns near the Plaza de Cataluñya more than a year ago while battling the Spanish Nationalist Army. His remains had been cremated against the wishes of the church and of his own family. Gabriela, always headstrong, had not decided on his burial site even as she planned to leave Barcelona for an unknown destination. His ashes were in a sealed copper container that rarely left her sight.

She was worried about her son's future birthdays and the edict of compulsory military service, so she was constantly reading the few newspapers she could find for the latest government's bulletin.

While they were mulling their plans to leave the city, an errant bomb hit the café-meson across the street and left a gaping gray-black hole, not only where the restaurant had been, but on the street itself, which made passage impossible. It was then that Gabriela, with the help of Fernando and Teresa, packed their belongings and left the *barrio* on foot to secure lodging in a safer place. They planned on going to a modest dwelling in the Raval district owned by a close family friend, Martín Revente. For the time being, it would have to do, since they had not obtained visas to leave for any other country. There existed the possibility of obtaining passage on a ship in the Barcelona port, if they could manage to buy tickets for the ever-decreasing spaces available on outgoing vessels. In addition, transportation would have to include any ocean-worthy ship that could take them to America. Don Martín would help them, since he had contacts in the shipping lines and ticket offices, being a retired Ports Authority official.

* * *

Two months after leaving their *Barrio Gótico* home, news came to the Díaz family that Barcelona had fallen, and that the only obstacle between the defeat of the Republican government and total victory by Franco's forces was the defense of Madrid. By February 1939, more than a half a million soldiers of the Republican Army had already fled across the French border, and the government there had set up camps to house all the refugees. On March 31, 1939, Madrid fell; the Spanish Civil War was essentially over.

Gabriela's family savings were in peril. Augustin Roche, her grandfather and family scion, had left funds in a Swiss bank which could secure her family's passage north to France, be it with a trek to the Spanish-French border or by a vessel to Marseilles. It was her choice, and information received from friends and relatives indicated that the trek north to the border was fraught with danger. Reports had it that refugees, both civilian and military, were being gunned down by the Condor Legion, in spite of the fact that the deserters from the Republican military were no longer fighting.

* * *

"Mamá, what are we waiting for?" Fernando asked.

"We are waiting for the right moment. You've heard the news, people are being killed by the fascists, even as they flee with nothing but their personal items," Gabriela replied.

"Isn't it more dangerous to stay here?"

"I'm working on that. Now leave me be."

"It's getting worse by the day. They will kill us all."

"As I said, I'm going to get us out. *Por favor calla ya.*"

* * *

Gabriela couldn't help but see her children as desperate, fatherless, and not able to grow up in peace in their own country. The choices were grim. Either a dangerous attempt to flee north with clogged roads, thousands of refugees, and air raids that were nonstop even with the fall of Barcelona, or stay put. The more she waited, the worse it became to travel to the French border; this she fully realized. Food was scarce: bread was almost nonexistent, rations were strictly enforced, meat and vegetables were prized like gold. The population was starving, and in one act of cruel mockery, Franco's Air Force dropped loaves of bread on the streets from up high, to show their feigned sympathy for the hunger being suffered by the Catalonians. Propaganda at its best.

Don Martín came through for her, and for an enormous amount of pesetas, she bought three one-way tickets to depart Barcelona on April 14th, 1939; first to Marseilles, then later to the Caribbean. However, in order to get on the Marseilles vessel, she would have to hire a local fisherman to take the family outside of the port, from a small wharf in Barceloneta, on the fringe of the city. This vessel would take them to a French ship, the *Duquesne*, which awaited. This was planned to avoid being detained by the Nationalist forces. The new port officers were inspecting and screening every departing passenger. She was the widow of a former Republican Army officer, and this fact was commonly known. His funeral had been well attended by his comrades, and by a group from a coalition which included communists, anarchists, and American fighters from the Lincoln Brigade.

Gabriela made one last visit to her mother, Penélope, now 84, yet still elegant in her manner, to say farewell and see if she could convince her to come with them to France, if not all the way to Puerto Rico. Gabriela would make plans for her later, if her mother agreed to leave.

"*Niña, estoy muy vieja y no sobreviviría el viaje.* I won't survive the journey."

"*Mamá, no es verdad.* You are strong and healthy. You can do it. The trip has become easier with the new ships that cross the Atlantic.

We can board the SS *Habana* in Marseilles. Or you can remain in France for a short period of time."

"Then you would have to bury me once we reach Puerto Rico, no?"

Gabriela knew it was not going to work. Penélope would die in Barcelona, never having visited her brother Antonio in Puerto Rico, where he had remained for the rest of his life.

* * *

Don Martín came down to the cellar bedroom that he had arranged for the Díaz family and awoke Gabriela at midnight on April 6th.

"You must be prepared to leave early tomorrow at 5 in the morning. They have tightened the restrictions on departures and are on the lookout for anyone sympathizing with the Republicans, and that includes immediate family. If they stop you, they will put you and the children in detention for a long time and will confiscate your passports and other documents. You must leave now." His voice was hoarse and weak, which only made him sound all the more terrifying.

"But our tickets say April 14th, won't they refuse to let us board?" Gabriela asked quietly so as not to wake the children.

"I've taken care of that with my friend, another port official, who has contacted the ship's captain. They had plans to leave earlier anyway, because they are at full capacity. But they have made room for all of you. Remember you are leaving from Barceloneta, not the large port. I will take you there myself."

"How can we ever thank you, Martín?"

"Don't worry, I'll find a way. Maybe you can thank me if I ever make it to America."

Gabriela had hoped to pack a few suitcases for the family, but her plans were dashed when Don Martín told her that it would be one suitcase for her, and just a large one for both children. Nothing more.

She gasped at the thought. *Two suitcases for the entire family?* Not what she was accustomed to. That meant that every item of her fine clothes would be left behind, as would the children's best outfits. *How could she survive?*

A volley of gunfire at the end of the block jarred her back to reality. There wasn't any choice to be made. Leave Barcelona or stay behind. The streets were clogged with fleeing Catalonians, and vandalism took hold of the once sedate and quiet alleyways of the *Barrio Gótico*. Storefront windows were smashed in a haphazard manner on major boulevards, and many homes had been broken into by fleeing mobs, while the criminal element had taken advantage of the disorder.

Don Martín told her that the Republican government had fled, after destroying as many official documents that they had time for, which might have included her marriage certificate and her children's birth documents. Luckily, she and the children had their own passports, product of their family trips to Biarritz, France for summer holidays. Those were in better times, she recalled.

That morning in the dark, Gabriela awakened Fernando and Teresa, both of whom resisted with protests and questions.

"Ask no questions, children. We are leaving ahead of time. I'll explain later. *Nos vamos ahora, apúrense,*" Gabriela urged.

"But we haven't packed yet, Mamá."

"I did it for you last night while you slept. Please hurry."

Don Martín had an old grayish rust colored Hispano-Suiza sedan, circa 1927, more like a station wagon than anything else, and he drove them to Barceloneta, following the Paseo de La Rambla to its end, then taking a less congested route to get to the Paseo Maritimo de la Barceloneta, the departure point. It was there, on a black rusted steel pier, that Gabriela and the children would board a fishing vessel to take them to the larger ship, the *Duquesne*.

Once there, they remained inside the sedan to avoid a passing truck filled with infantrymen from Franco's army. After it passed, they walked rapidly to an empty warehouse to wait for the fishermen's crew. A solitary private watchman stopped them at the entrance and asked them what their business was at that early hour. Don Martín had decided to wait for the family to board the fishing boat and saw the sentry approach Gabriela and the children. They remained silent with puzzled looks on their faces. He walked up behind the man, who had reached for his whistle to call for help. At that moment, Don Martín took out a small heavy leather club and hit the man on the head with brute force. The blow knocked out the sentry.

It was time to run. Gabriela took off her high-heeled shoes and ran barefoot to the boat named *La Catalana Loca*, moored right off the dock. The children followed quickly. Before going onboard, she bid goodbye to Don Martín, kissing him on both cheeks and asking, "Why are you doing all these kind things for us?"

"*Mi señora*, Lieutenant Díaz saved my life once. If not for him, I wouldn't be here."

Gabriela didn't have the chance to ask what her husband had done. She went aboard the boat, turned around and shouted, "Come see us in Puerto Rico. You will have a home there. I promise!"

He smiled and nodded, then waved goodbye as the vessel removed its rope lines from the dock and left.

* * *

The waters were choppy and the *Catalana* swayed from side to side, sometimes appearing that it would capsize, but was finally able to make it to the *Duquesne*, after a struggle to get alongside the ship. Gabriela and the children were lucky enough that this vessel had a small swinging gangplank that permitted them to access the ship without much danger. Two sailors aboard the ship assisted them.

The fishing boat swung away from the ocean vessel and the crew waved *goodbye*. Gabriela stood near the stern of the ship. with Teresa and Fernando viewing the city of Barcelona perhaps for the last time. They could still see the famous Christopher Columbus statue facing west at the end of La Rambla. First tears welled up in the children's eyes, then as the tears flowed, they both hugged Gabriela. She also wept, reflecting the enormity of this sudden change in their lives, with no idea of what would happen to them on the voyage to the New World.

Chapter 2
Marseilles To San Juan

The *Duquesne*, built in the mid-1920s, was a ship that for its age handled well on the high seas. It had been a French Navy Cruiser for its first 10 years but was later converted to a passenger ship and its interior updated. The cabin that Gabriela paid for was small, with no porthole, well below deck, but did not suffer from some of the noises that permeated other parts of the ship's interior. It contained a small wash basin, one bunk bed, and a single bed on the opposite side of the room. It had once been used by French Naval officers. For other necessities, passengers had to go to common water closets on the same level in the ship's stern. Since the travel to Marseilles was less than a day, the accommodations would do, giving them time for some rest.

Many other passengers did not fare so well, since they were the poorest of refugees fleeing the fascist takeover. Some slept on the deck, while others didn't even bother. The experience had left them in full shock and disbelief and they couldn't sleep. The slightest noise would frighten them, and the noises were nonstop.

* * *

Gabriela walked on the deck to the stern with thoughts of Carmelo. How handsome he had looked in his uniform when the war began, and how tattered it was on the day he left for what would become his last battle for the Republic.

After a few miles out at sea, she walked the deck and stopped suddenly, opened her scarf, which had a small bag tied in a knot, and stretched her arm beyond the ship's banister. She pulled her arm back, opened the bag, and again reached out to scatter a portion of Carmelo's ashes in Spanish waters. The remainder of his ashes would be buried sometime later, perhaps in *Borinquen*.

She did not cry. All her tears for Carmelo had dried up long ago. She lingered on the memory of his kiss the last morning of his life, and on his final embrace.

After turning away from the sea, she noticed a man approaching her, dressed as a civilian, but in a suit not made in Spain as evidenced by its different cut of cloth. He stopped, said hello, and touched his hat. He smiled as he resumed his walk. Something about him intrigued Gabriela. His manner didn't appear that of a Spaniard. She walked to the bow, and as she passed by a group of passengers, she heard him speaking with an accent which she didn't hear often. It was Spanish, but pronounced without the famous lisp, or the cadences of the Catalonians. Almost musical, full of gaiety.

Was the accent from Galicia, the Canary Islands, or Cuba? she thought.

Later that afternoon she saw him again. She smiled this time, then paused in her stride and blurted out, "Where are you from, Cuba?" She instantly regretted the remark.

Surprised, he turned around. "I'm from Puerto Rico, in the Antilles."

"And what brought you to Barcelona?"

"I was on a school break and a vacation." He looked away as he said this.

"You're still in school?" Again, she regretted the remark and blushed.

"Yes. I'm specializing in my field. Orthopedics"

"I'm sorry, I didn't mean it that way."

"My name is Pedro Santana from San Juan. To whom do I have the pleasure of addressing, and who has so many questions without knowing me?"

"Gabriela Díaz Roche. I'm traveling, hopefully, to your *patria* at the end of this journey. My cousin and his family live in San Juan."

"What ship are you taking out of Marseilles?"

"I think it's the *Habana*."

"I'm headed to the island as well, but on a different ship, a few days from now. There is no way of knowing for sure how long it will take, with the way things are developing here in Europe, and the growing threats of war. I hope I don't have to wait long."

"So do I," she said.

"I had to reserve a place on a French ocean liner, which will stop briefly in New York, but continue on to San Juan, the *de France*. It's a newer and faster ship and saves me a few days of travel with only one stop. It normally leaves the port of Le Havre, near Paris, then goes on to New York, but it has been rerouted for that voyage. It's a nine-day journey, plus five or six more days from New York to the island," he added. "Are you traveling with family?"

"Yes, I am. With my children."

He remained silent for a moment, then said, "Well, it was nice speaking to you. Have a pleasant trip." He bowed slightly, then left her before she could ask him any more questions.

* * *

The *Duquesne* docked in Marseilles later that night, and the passengers who did not have reservations in nearby hotels were allowed to spend the first night aboard ship.

The port was impressive, with a domineering tower on the hill, high above the marina. The entrance to the port had a castle guarding it as ships approached; it was the front door to Provence. Many smaller fishing boats lined both sides of the U-shaped harbor. Gabriela found it peaceful.

She disembarked the next morning and went to the offices of the shipping lines at the port to inquire about the SS *Habana* and its departure date. No one seemed to know, then an official told her the ship had been delayed and would not arrive in Marseilles for another week.

"Exactly when next week?' Gabriela asked him as he kept on looking at a chart in his hands.

"Maybe Wednesday or Thursday. It says here in a telegram to our offices that it encountered a storm at sea during the crossing, which forced it to stop in the Canary Islands for repairs."

"Is there any ship that leaves sooner for New York or San Juan?" she asked.

"No."

That left Gabriela with no choice but to secure temporary lodging for the family. Most of the inns near the port were full. Pedestrian traffic at the port was teeming with passengers from all levels of society. Some wore ragtag clothes, others wore their best suits and dresses, but all fleeing Spain, the reason for the scarcity of rooms.

With the help of another port official, she found a small inn, *Le Boutique Maison,* three blocks away from the pier on a side street hidden from the main boulevard. The inn was clean, but there were no extra luxuries that Gabriela had to come to expect when traveling away from Barcelona.

Fernando looked around the room assigned to them. "*Mami*, are we supposed to stay here for one week?"

"*Si, mijo.* It's the best I could find."

"But where is the bathroom?" Teresa chimed in. She frowned and held her nose as she spoke.

"Just like the ship, in the rear, a common bath for all the rooms on this floor," Gabriela said.

"Ugh," Fernando said. "At least the ship was only for a few hours, not a whole week."

"*Basta ya.*" She touched her purse without thinking, as if reassuring herself that her funds would last the entire journey.

* * *

The week in Marseilles went fast; the city was welcoming, and in spite of the language barrier, they found the people kind and the food plentiful, mostly simple staples of seafood and vegetables, but all were nourishing. The inn only offered coffee and croissants for breakfast, lots of them, and the three of them splurged on the tasty morsels every day. In fact, the children looked forward to that morning meal since the croissants were sometimes filled with delicious chocolate.

As predicted, the SS *Habana* arrived in Marseilles in late April and was scheduled to depart in three days, on April 27th, for New York, Cuba, and then Puerto Rico.

Gabriela was filled with hope, while the children's anxiety seemed to fade as well. Fernando started imitating the French gestures. Teresa had picked up a few words herself. *Merci* was her favorite.

The day to board the ship arrived, and Gabriela and the children left for the port. The customs official there examined their temporary visitor passes and the vessel tickets and gave a cursory glance at their luggage.

"*Bon voyage*," he said in a desultory manner and waved them on. Gabriela nodded, and Teresa replied with her new favorite French word.

Once aboard the *Habana*, they found the ship was designed for Atlantic crossings, and built better than the *Duquesne*. Gabriela breathed a sigh of relief that perhaps this was the beginning of a newer and improved chapter of their lives.

They proceeded to their assigned cabin, which had a medium-sized porthole. Gabriela had made sure of that for a nine-day Atlantic crossing to New York, plus the additional days to the Caribbean.

As she walked on deck, she overheard passengers talk about war seeming inevitable, since Hitler had made menacing threats against Poland and its allies.

She stumbled into Pedro Santana, who expressed no surprise in seeing her, and had almost missed her as he opened the dining room door. Outside, he greeted her like an old friend.

"Well, here we meet again, Señora...I forget your name, *perdona*."

"Gabriela Díaz. I didn't forget yours, Doctor Santana."

He raised his eyebrows, looking surprised at her good memory of their brief encounter.

"May I ask why you are traveling on this ship?" she said.

"The *de France* won't be coming to Marseilles after all, It has been held up in Paris due to the gathering war clouds."

"I heard the same rumors."

"So now we have time to become friends.

" He paused, then added, "How is your family? I never met your children, or your husband."

"My children are fine. You will see them during the trip. I'm a war widow. My husband was killed in 1937, fighting Franco's army."

"*Lo siento, no lo sabía*. My deepest condolences."

"*Gracias*. I must go now and fetch my son and daughter."

"How old are they?"

"Fernando is 14, almost 15, and Teresa is 13."

Something in the manner in which he stated his regrets, made her feel that he really wasn't on vacation in Spain. He was older, probably married with children, and did not seem like a person spending his vacation in a war-torn country. She was curious and vowed to find out. But that conversation would have to wait until they had settled in, if indeed she met him again in the proper setting. Gabriela didn't want to embarrass herself again by asking personal questions.

* * *

Pedro Santana was born in the outskirts of Caguas, Puerto Rico in 1903, and came from a humble family living just off old Highway 1. He had made a name for himself in his years practicing medicine. Married quite young, father of one child, Pedro later separated and divorced his wife, Sylvia Lastra, in 1935. This was seven years after his graduation from medical school at the University of Puerto Rico.

General medicine was fine for him for a time and he thrived, but he had it in his mind to become a specialist, an orthopedic surgeon. At the time, the choice was either going to the United States to study in a renowned university there, or go to Madrid, which was much less expensive. The choice was easy, and the medical school at the Central University of Madrid was very flexible with the timelines they set for students to finish a specialty. He could go to school for a semester, return to Puerto Rico, skip a semester, then return. The plan worked for the first two years, then the Civil War broke out in Spain. He was stranded there, with the medical school closing in early 1938, and him unable to return home.

At the onset of the conflict, Santana remained neutral in his political sympathies, but as the war dragged on, with no easy victories as the Republican government had predicted, he grew fond of the resistance by the Loyalists to Franco's army rebellion, especially after he heard stories of the atrocities committed by the latter.

He relocated to Barcelona when it appeared that the medical school wouldn't reopen anytime soon, and made plans for a short vacation, which later morphed into semi-volunteer work at a hospital for the wounded Republican Army soldiers. The compensation was meager—a small stipend, food, and shelter. But Pedro enjoyed the camaraderie and the morale of the men recovering from their wounds. He loved their conversations of how they planned to return to battle, all the while drinking unlimited amounts of wine.

It was then in 1939 that he decided to return to Puerto Rico after almost two years of army surgical work in Loyalist field hospitals. That type of information he kept to himself, so when he met Gabriela, he didn't reveal his past work with the Republicans.

He was slightly built, with reddish blond hair, light brown eyes, and freckles, which made people mistake him for a Scotsman or an Irishman. He laughed at those comments.

As he began the voyage on the *Habana* and reflected on his

encounter with Gabriela, he asked himself what, if anything, he would reveal to this young attractive widow. He was dazzled by her beauty— her hazel eyes, radiant skin, tight figure, amazing long black hair—but had tried to not show it.

His mind was also full of thoughts on his aborted specialization studies, but he found comfort at the thought of reopening his practice in Caguas, and possibly finding a new love interest.

* * *

He had several encounters with Gabriela on the westbound crossing of the Atlantic, and he was beginning to grow fond of her, as well as her two well behaved children. She spoke about her deceased Uncle Antonio and the growth of his businesses, but focused more on her cousin Carlos, who was now in charge of the family businesses, a liquor distillery producing high quality rum, and a cement factory.

One evening during dinner with her, he spoke about the history of the ship they were on.

"Did you know that this is the same ship that in 1937 transported to London hundreds of small children, who were being evacuated from the Basque countries?"

"No, I did not. This same ship, the *Habana*?"

"Yes, and my prediction it that many of those children growing up in England will not return to Spain once they become adults."

"That seems possible, I guess. I'm not sure how things will work out for me in Puerto Rico. I do have family there, but there is a real chance we might not return to Spain. I shudder when those thoughts cross my mind. I loved Barcelona and our way of life. At least the way it used to be."

"It will never be the same, I fear. But new adventures await you in Puerto Rico. The best thing about humans is our ability to adjust."

"Sounds like the doctor in you."

The rest of the meal was spent with little talk, but they eyed each other when they thought the other one was not looking.

* * *

The *Habana* arrived in New York on the morning of May 9th and anchored at the Red Hook Pier in Brooklyn on its first stop. There was no need for the passengers to disembark if they were continuing on the voyage to the Caribbean, since the ship would stay in port for only 12 hours before sailing again.

To the surprise of many passengers, the ship did not go directly to Cuba, as previously announced, but would first stop in San Juan, six days later. Many passengers heading to Cuba objected to the change, but the detour would delay their arrival in Havana by only two days according to the ship's officials, so they relented.

Upon arrival in San Juan, they were told that the reason for the change in itinerary was an emergency stop to obtain a spare part for the ship's engines, which the Havana port no longer carried. Very few passengers believed this, but only a few protested.

The beauty of the San Juan harbor and the majestic entrance of El Morro fortress, which was quite similar to the Spanish fort in Havana harbor, helped calm some of the passengers' anxiety.

* * *

In their last dinner before disembarking, Pedro asked Gabriela if she had an address so that he could someday write her a note. She agreed and read it from a piece of paper she carried in her purse. The Roches, her family, had moved from their house on the Condado lagoon, and resided now on Magdalena Avenue, in the center of an area known as El Condado.

"I wish you a pleasant relocation on the island. You will find it different from Barcelona, but just as lively and invigorating, and most of all you will hear music and laughter everywhere you go."

She smiled. "My hope is that we will meet again," Gabriela said. They did not kiss goodbye in the Spanish fashion, but did shake hands, which he found odd.

Chapter 3
The Arrival

On May 1st, 1939, the passengers of the SS *Habana* disembarked in the port of San Juan. Those passengers headed for Cuba would remain on board and not go through customs since their ultimate destination was Cuba. They could leave the ship for a short period of time if they chose, using temporary visitor's passes issued by the ship and validated by the local authorities.

Gabriela and her children were among the last to leave the ship. She was in no rush to do so, since her cousin, Carlos Roche Soler, would meet them at the pier and take them to his residence. They would live there until they could find suitable quarters.

On her way towards the gangplank, someone tapped her shoulder from behind.

"I guess this is where we say goodbye for now, *señora*."

Gabriela turned around and tried to hide her surprise, but only succeeded at not blushing for too long once she saw Pedro.

"*Si, verdad.* Hope you find your family well, Doctor. *Adiós.*"

"Call me Pedro, please."

"*Bien.* Pedro."

He bent over and kissed her right cheek lightly. She didn't respond, but later touched it self-consciously, assuring herself she was not imagining this gesture. She reflected on how handsome he was, so well-mannered, and perfectly tailored.

"*Hasta pronto,*" he said, and waved goodbye. She watched him disappear down the long wharf and head to the buildings which flanked the Calle Recinto Sur of Old San Juan. He walked briskly as if he were trying to not miss a train. She soon lost sight of him.

Teresa pulled on her arm to indicate her wish to leave the ship. Fernando was waiting for them at the exit of the down ramp.

As they disembarked, a long black Ford sedan drove up, stopped, and out of the driver's seat jumped Carlos Roche. A woman, who Gabriela later found out was his second wife, María Antonia Roche, emerged from the passenger side. They walked rapidly towards the family.

Before entering the car with the children, Gabriela stopped to take in her surroundings. The New World, the New Spain and its former colony of Puerto Rico, now an American possession. A new beginning for her and for so many of her countrymen after a devastating and tragic civil war.

The architecture was not strictly Spanish; it had colonial vestiges in the color of the houses, which had elaborate entryways and carefully carved stone steps. The streets were paved with ship's ballast serving as blue gray cobblestones, a feature she had not seen since childhood. The shades of color in the buildings were mostly pastel, including bright pinks, yellows, greens, and peacock blues.

There were palm trees and flowers everywhere. The stone and mortar walls of ancient forts bordered the old city. On their way to El Condado, they crossed a bridge with striking views of the ocean and the adjoining green and azure lagoon.

Mostly, Old San Juan seemed to have the peace they longed for.

* * *

Carlos and María Antonia Roche had married and adjusted to a stable home life after the final turbulent years of the 1930s. Business seemed to be prospering, since their jointly held interest in a rum distillery and in a cement factory provided steady sources of income. Carlos was an executive in both industries. The new decade had promised a bright future for Puerto Rico, with sweeping changes in the political makeup of the island's legislature.

The two had moved to Magdalena Street 150 in the Condado, to a residence that had been in disrepair when purchased. It was remodeled, painted a soft pearly white, and the roof tiles had been replaced by bright red ones, which gave it an Andalusian flair. The twin faux towers on the roof and wrought iron window grates were the finishing touches. A new cement driveway had been laid, which spanned from the entrance gate up to the kitchen side door. The main iron gate, painted black, replicated the original portal at the Roche mansion in Barcelona.

"I trust you will be comfortable here with us for the time being," Carlos said to Gabriela and the two children after they had reached the newly restored home. "You have a choice of the two upper bedrooms or separate living quarters at the end of the driveway, which has its own kitchen and bathroom. Also, you will soon meet my daughter Ana, who is now visiting her mother in Ponce."

"You are too generous, Carlos. *Gracias,* María Antonia," Gabriela said.

Teresa and Fernando were surprised with the accommodations, and the astonished look on their faces when they entered the separate guest house convinced their mother to choose that for their stay.

The climate was pleasant, with temperatures in the low 80's, a change from Barcelona in the early spring. *Cruces de Malta* were blooming in the front yard, and a large Flamboyan tree gave distinction to the property.

Carlos made the entire house available for their inspection and told the hired help that they were to treat the new arrivals as family.

Gabriela took a moment and sat down on the bed to let this new experience sink in. The children went to inspect the backyard and play with the house dog, *Chispita*, a black and white terrier mix.

Carlos offered the Díaz's a light lunch since he had to leave for his office, then spoke to Gabriela with María Antonia listening.

"You will find everything you need here, and if not, just ask. I know you will learn to love this island and San Juan as my father and mother did. It has a way of growing on you. Not as developed or as sophisticated as Barcelona or Madrid, but nevertheless with a bright future, especially since we expect to win the next elections handily," Carlos said.

"Who is we?" Gabriela asked.

"The new political party, the Popular Democrats."

"That's what you think," María Antonia interjected with a feigned smile.

"Just wait and see. November is only 18 months away," Carlos replied.

"You don't belong to the same political groups?" Gabriela asked in a surprised tone.

"No, we don't, but that's enough politics, Carlos. They just arrived." María Antonia gave him a gentle push towards the door.

He bid his goodbye after once again emphasizing his welcome to the new family members and then left.

* * *

Ana Roche Rodríguez, Carlos' daughter, almost nine years old, had lived through the death of her brother, Toñito, at the hands of the National Guard and police in 1937, but the years had not fully erased that memory or the manner in which he died. Margarita Rodríguez, her mother, had suffered a mental breakdown after that loss, and now lived in the house of her parents, who were elderly and retired. She was under constant care with a live-in nurse.

Ana didn't particularly care much for her father's new wife, and avoided spending too much time with María Antonia, thus her frequent trips to Ponce.

She was too young to have any serious political leanings, but she admired her mother and all the sacrifices she had made pursuing her ideals. Too many, she thought, certainly not worth her brother's life. However, the future might prove her mother right. As a young girl, studying in a private Catholic girl's school in San Juan, she didn't have much time to dwell on this topic, at least for the present.

Ana was slender and quite tall for her age. Thin like a model, with the same type and color hair as her mother, but cut a bit shorter, she had an elegant walk and held her carriage erect at all times, as if she were practicing for a fashion runway. Her dark brown hair made her stand out, and she wore it in braids while at school. Her eyes were hazel, complimenting her tan. *Trigueña* was her color, a light caramel. She had inherited those genes from her grandfather, Jacinto Rodríguez, which indicated a Taino ancestor somehow, or so she was told.

The middle school, Our Lady of Immaculada Academy, was located not too far from El Condado, on Ponce de Leon Ave, near the old trolley Stop 26. It was run by nuns of the Dominican order, who imposed their own brand of discipline, sometimes far stricter than most parents. She resented this, and was outspoken about it, which frequently landed her in the Mother Superior's office.

Mother Caridad had a weak spot for Ana, knowing fully well her family history; she was very warm and understanding with her, different from most of the school staff. But she wasn't as lenient with other students in trouble.

"What did you do today to upset your teacher, *cariño?*" Mother Caridad asked.

"*Nada.* Nothing. Sister Dolores is always picking on me, and she ignores others when they break the rules."

"Remember dear, she is older, and at her age she gets upset quickly, since her patience is wearing thin. She is hard of hearing as well. Please try to understand that."

"She should retire to a convent in Spain. All I did was pass a note to the student behind me, the only friend I have here."

Ana bit her lip after saying that and started squirming, but soon tears welled up in her eyes. The nun gave her time to compose herself.

"Please my dear. Go back and apologize, tomorrow is another day." Ana rose, forced a smile, and left.

Ana returned from Ponce home the same afternoon that the Díaz family arrived, and she met the new family from Barcelona. They had just moved in, she was told. She hoped they were not Spanish snobs; her school was already full of them. Since the two children were close to her age, perhaps she could make friends with her distant cousins.

"*Hola. Bienvenidos a Puerto Rico,*" Ana said upon meeting them. She hugged them both, as was the custom.

"*Gracias,*" they both replied in unison.

After asking them a few questions about their voyage, she said to them, "Later, I would like to take you both for a walk at a nearby park. It's not very big, but it's beautiful and quiet. Just a short distance from here."

"*Vale,*" they said.

She found Fernando very young, but masculine and attractive, and thought that the girl, Teresa, was very attentive, if not actually pretty.

As they walked around the small plaza in the park, they asked her questions about life on the island. Ana was not too familiar with Fernando's interests, but was able to discern Teresa's attraction to nature and her surroundings.

"And what do you like to do, Fernando?" Ana asked.

"Sports. *Balonpie*, futbol, or as the Americanos say, Soccer."

"Have you played before?"

"Yes, I was on my school team. I played the striker position, and I was pretty good."

"He's also very humble," Teresa added.

"And you Teresa, what do you like to do?"

"I plan to be a writer. I read almost anything. And someday I will write a novel."

They returned to the house on Magdalena after a one-hour stroll around the neighborhood.

Fernando and Teresa had arrived in May, at the end of the school year, so they couldn't enter junior high school until mid-August, but Gabriela made sure they were enrolled in a summer session that was offered by some private schools. She chose English as one of the first subjects to be taught to her children.

* * *

Carlos kept busy in his two simultaneous occupations, but found time to tinker in the political arena. Plans for next year's island-wide elections were in full swing, and he had accepted a part-time position in the governing board of the Populares party, at the request of Luis Muñoz Marín, who was its recognized leader. While he didn't have daily contact with Muñoz, he remained in touch through phone calls and short notes.

María Antonia, on the other hand, was active in promoting women's rights, and had been instrumental in the island campaign for the right to vote, which had been successful. She remained a steadfast member of the Statehood Republican Party and considered joining the national organization.

As far as Carlos could ascertain, the only serious challenge to his group were the Republicans, and to some extent, the extremists of the independence movement, many whom were followers of the Nationalist Party led by Pedro Albizu Campos. The latter group wanted a complete separation from the United States by any means necessary, even if by violence. They were unpredictable. He would never forget what this group had done that led to the death of his son, Toñito.

His former wife, Margarita Rodríguez, had remained tied to the ideal of Independence, notwithstanding the loss of her only son. Carlos heard that at night she would scream Toñito's name repeatedly, and call for him, as if he were lost.

Chapter 4
The New Borinquen

Vicente Ferrer passed away in 1942 at age 78 before he could finish his work at restoring the family coffee farm in Sabana Grande. He had done his best to make his farm profitable, but he hadn't quite accomplished it at the end of his days.

His son, Gregorio, now a father in his own right, had married Monserrate Perez from Yauco, Puerto Rico. They had given birth to three sons, Juan, Edwin, and Daniel, and a daughter, Christina. Gregorio had taken over management of the coffee farm from Vicente, and for a while it seemed that the production of coffee might be restored to its former self. He then passed most of the responsibility for operations first to Juan, who didn't particularly want them, then to Edwin, due to the onset of an illness that would affect his health and shorten his life. He had developed heart failure, his doctor said.

But Edwin, by age 23, had grown tired of harvesting coffee and longed for a brighter future, especially with the island-wide victories of the Populares in 1940. There was hope now that a new age was dawning. While his own family was not among the poorest of the town, they had some basic needs, and the coffee farm, although partially recovering from hurricanes (and from an embezzlement perpetuated by a former family friend and colleague, Felix Prats) did not provide a secure future for the family.

There was hope that new industries coming to the island, known as the "Poor House of the Caribbean," would change this. The newly founded political party had promised land reform and jobs for as many as were willing to work in these industries, once the jobs were created. But the truth was that there just weren't enough jobs for all, not with the problem of overpopulation.

Edwin sought a different path, one that would lead to a better future. He was at a crossroads; he was still single, and he couldn't really leave the household since his mother might soon become a widow. Juan was more interested in women than in coffee. Daniel, at 15, wasn't old enough to manage a farm, and Christina, 13, lived in another world, a fantasy one. Edwin realized he needed to wait for the right moment to begin life in a different place. His education was limited, only up to the 10th grade, but he had ambitions to at least finish high school, even if he had to attend classes at night.

Another hope was that the war in Europe and in the Pacific would end at some point, and life would return to normal, whatever that might be. He had read in the island newspapers that several German submarines had been sunk north of the island by the U.S. Navy, with the assistance of Puerto Rican sailors, who were familiar with that part of the Atlantic. Before 1942, these submarines had been a threat to ongoing shipping between Puerto Rico and the mainland. In fact, the war had put on hold the ambitious plans of land and economic reform for the island. A new *Borinquen* had been promised, but world conflict and local politics had paused its creation for the time being. This pause included Edwin's plans as well.

At the end of the war in Europe in May 1945, plans by the government were initiated for what would be known as Operation Bootstrap, a modern economic development formula for the island and its people. It would be adopted sometime in 1947, with promises of massive industrialization.

Edwin considered those plans and realized there was no place for him there. He didn't want to spend the rest of his working life in a farm or a factory. He wanted more.

A tall figure was not one of his traits. In fact, he was rather short for a man, only 5 feet 6 inches, but had a muscular physique and dark brown eyes that matched his medium brown-reddish hair. He was not really handsome, but somehow attracted people by being articulate, by his demeanor, and how he socialized with others. He had met many women in his short life, but only one had really grabbed his attention. No other one, not even the young woman he lost his virginity to. But there was one that caught his fancy, one he had first seen at a town *verbena*, a town fair, in the Puerto Rican tradition, where many vendors displayed their wares, mostly typical island food. There were musicians playing many Puerto Rican tunes, with a few couples dancing in the plaza square in front of the church.

The young woman he saw one evening in the plaza was fair haired with blue eyes and just about his size. He could hear her laugh across the park, where men strolled around in one direction and women walked in the opposite. In this way, he passed her often in circular walks around the perimeter of the park.

A friend from his *barrio*, Carmela Soto, offered to introduce the young woman to him, and he accepted.

Laura Ríos smiled when he approached her with Carmela and she offered her hand in a delicate manner. He took her hand but did not actually shake it. He then gently let go.

"I'm Edwin Ferrer, at your service. *Es un placer.*"

"Mine as well," she said. "*Soy Laura.*"

Now up close, he saw that her blue eyes were her most captivating feature, along with her dirty blond hair. He tried not to stare.

They had a brief conversation, and then each resumed their own separate strolls.

"Carmela, is she single? Does she have a *novio?*"

"Not that I know, Edwin. But I imagine she has a few suitors."

"Where does she live?"

"On Betances street, just off the plaza, with her family."

"I assume she's in school? "

"Yes, she's a freshman at the university."

Edwin gulped when he heard the answer.

"You mean the UPR? But she looks like a high school student."

"Laura is so intelligent that she skipped her senior year of high school and got into college early. She comes home every weekend from Rio Piedras, in a *público*. She wants to become a teacher someday."

Edwin stopped asking questions, since clearly Laura seemed out of his league. He said goodbye to Carmela and returned home to the farm, both inspired and depressed.

Monserrate, his mother, noticed his mood.

"*Que te pasa?*" What's wrong, Edwinsito?"

"Nothing, *nada*. I'm 23, have no future, and just met an angel who is the loveliest woman I have ever seen, *es preciosa*."

"Well don't be a *bobo*, do something. Something that won't upset her or her parents, *esta bien?*"

"*Okey.*"

Edwin asked Carmela for Laura's address to send her a note. He hesitated, but a week later wrote to her, not expecting a reply. One came anyway, to his surprise. In his note he had asked if he could visit her at home, at her convenience, and she had agreed.

They met on a Sunday afternoon at her home. After church Mass was the best time, before she left for school.

He dressed in his best clothes, usually saved for weddings, baptisms, or funerals and appeared at her house on Betances Street at 2:00 p.m. Edwin climbed the short steps to the front veranda and knocked on the massive brown wooden door.

An older man answered. "And who are you?"

"Edwin Ferrer, here to see Laura Ríos, at her request."

Edwin glanced at the floor. He had fudged the answer to indicate he would be welcome.

"Stay here, I'll call her. I'm her father, Arnaldo Ríos." They didn't shake hands.

A few minutes later Laura appeared in a light blue cotton dress which almost matched her eyes. She invited him to sit down on a small sofa on the porch, while she sat in a separate chair.

"We didn't get to speak much when we met. That's why I'm here," he said.

"I know. I've heard a lot about you from Carmela, so I don't feel like I'm speaking to a stranger."

"Well, I know nothing about you, except that you are studying at the UPR and want to become a teacher."

"Or a lawyer," she injected.

Edwin gulped again, harder this time.

"And you?" she continued. "What are your plans?"

He looked at the floor again before answering. *Good question, he thought.*

"I won't be a coffee farmer forever. I plan to finish school, and if I have to go to elsewhere to seek an opportunity, I will. I have a dream of having my own business someday. Not sure what that will be. But I may have to wait. My father is not well, and he can't handle the farm by himself, like my grandfather did."

"Do you have any pastimes?" Laura asked.

"Yes, I do. I play the guitar sometimes, and I like baseball. And you?"

"I sew much of what I wear, and I'm not a bad cook, but only when I feel like it, not every day like my mother, and certainly not three meals a day. I also tinker with the piano." She paused, then added, "You live on the road to Maricao, right?"

"Yes. The view up there is magnificent. You should visit."

They talked for almost three hours, and by then Edwin was smitten with her. Laura rose to indicate that their time was up. He rose, then said a few words about meeting again; she nodded but didn't reply.

Edwin looked back and noticed that she remained at the front door until he was almost out of sight. He hoped he'd made a good impression.

* * *

Laura had met many young men in high school and now in college, but none of them had that earnest look about them, or meaningful sincerity in their words. Almost all of them had marriage or something else on their mind, but not her.

She had plans for her future, and having a steady boyfriend was not part of them now, but she was attracted to this modest country boy who nevertheless looked full of life. His laugh was different. Genuine.

* * *

The hoped-for industrial modernization of the island came slowly after 1947, and the many plans to improve the agricultural development, manufacturing, and the sewing industries started at a snail's pace.

Employment conditions improved for sure, but not in a manner that made Edwin consider applying for that type of work. He thought about Laura every day during the weekdays when she was in Rio Piedras and waited anxiously for the weekends to see if they could meet. It couldn't be every weekend; she had to study and frequently met with a close group of friends from nearby towns, who studied at the Mayaguez campus of the UPR.

Edwin had nothing in common with those friends. The one time he met with Laura and them, he felt totally uncomfortable and didn't even try to make new acquaintances or start a conversation, contrary to his nature.

Dating without a chaperone was impossible. Carmela, their mutual friend, had her own social circle, and wasn't always available to fill in. Laura had no siblings, and her parents never left the house.

One day, about three months after they first met, they ran into each other at the local pharmacy. Edwin tapped her on the back. She spun around, saw him, and smiled.

"Laura," he started, "I have begun studying at night and hope to finish my high school in less than two years. Then I'll be ready to decide what to do."

"At least you have a plan. That's good." She hugged him and he was a bit startled. In reply, he kissed her cheek. She laughed.

Laura's parents were not too fond of Edwin, mainly due to his occupation and social status, but knew better than to try to interfere, or worse yet, forbid their friendship. They knew the latter action was impossible to enforce, and just hoped the liaison would die a natural death and not blossom into a courtship. In that regard, they were miles ahead of other small-town families who watched their young daughters like hawks and enforced rules that were often ignored by their offspring with bad results.

By the end of their first year of dating, on and off, they were more than friends, and their kisses reflected that. This unlikely pairing carried with it many risks. They were from different levels of society in town, a small community where everyone knew each other and each other's business.

One Sunday afternoon, Edwin broached a subject he had been avoiding—his plans to visit New York City. Migration of many Puerto Ricans to that city had already begun and he knew some friends and relatives living there.

He looked at Laura, who had a quizzical look at his uneasiness.

"Laura, I'm planning to visit New York City in the summer, to see all that I've heard. It won't be a short trip, maybe a month or a little more. I'll stay with a cousin from Gúanica who lives in the Lower East Side. Just for a visit, but I'm also going to see if there might be a future there for someone like me with very little school."

"You mean limited education, Edwin."

"Yes, that's right."

"Can you afford a trip like that?"

"The new way to get there is to fly, and Pan American offers tickets on a late-night flight for only 52 dollars."

"What about the farm?"

"I hired one of the workers to handle things. I'll pay him a little more money. Juan can't do it alone, not when he disappears two or three days at a time."

"Can you trust either of them? Look what happened to your grandfather when he went to prison, from what you have told me."

"*Claro*, if not, I wouldn't go."

"I'll miss you, Edwinsito."

"I don't like that nickname."

"Too bad. You are my Edwinsito, and that's that."

He forced a smile, then laughed politely.

"A month is a long time. But you will come back, won't you?" She said this with doubt in her voice.

"*Si, mi amor.*"

Edwin left her house thinking, *what if I wanted to stay longer? What if I found a good job? Would she really wait?*

Laura was a catch, many young men in the town were interested in her, and if he left her alone for too long, he could very well lose her. *What should I do? Leave and take my chances, shorten the trip, or just forget about New York?*

He had many sleepless nights struggling with this decision. But he decided to go to New York anyway. If he lost her affection in one month, then it wasn't meant to be. Sad as that thought was, he knew he would have to deal with it. He had many misgivings, since he really loved her.

* * *

Laura dwelled on the conversation they had just had, and though she was extremely fond of Edwin, she wasn't ready to make a commitment, not at her age, and not considering her plans. Many students had flirted with her on campus, and she felt that this was not the time to close any doors. If Edwin left, she wasn't going to sit idly by and wait for his return.

* * *

Edwin had to choose the right time to tell Laura when he made his decision. He would wait until May. He figured he would leave for the States in June and return sometime in mid-July. Even better, if he had a fixed return date in mind, it might make it easier to break the news to her even though he had no plane ticket to return.

He approached Laura on a Friday evening at home, and when they were on the porch, he asked her to sit and listen to what he had to say.

"You mean you are really going to make this crazy trip, for no other reason than to see a big city? What will I do while you are gone?"

Unexpectedly, her eyes started moistening, and she looked over his head at the pedestrian street traffic.

Edwin didn't expect her reaction and felt the blood rise in his cheeks. Something had changed since he first broached the idea.

"It's only a month, Laura. Please understand, I have to do this. Classes will be out for the summer and it's the perfect time."

"For you. What if I told you that the university has begun summer trips for students to visit Europe, beginning this summer, and they last for six weeks?"

"I would say go for it," he lied, still feeling the heat in his face.

"I don't believe you. So I'll tell you the truth. You don't know what you really want, and one month or two won't make a difference. So decide now, because I'm not going to sit here and wait for you until you come back. I don't want you to go, but if you do, then I'll do my own thing."

He was stunned, and for a moment speechless before he managed, "That's not what you said when I first told you about my plans."

"But that is what I'm saying now," Laura said angrily.

That couldn't be the real reason she was upset. Was there someone or something else going on?

An awkward silence took over. They avoided looking at each other.

"Is there something you don't want to tell me, Laura?"

"Nothing, Edwin. But I'm young and can't promise you anything. You realize that we live in different worlds, right?"

Those words stung Edwin. He knew that but assumed love would make those barriers disappear.

"Why did you wait until now to say that? We've been dating for one year. I thought you loved me too."

"I do. I'm very fond of you, but our whole life is in front of us. Can't we remain good friends just for now?"

He looked at her. She avoided his eyes and showed no visible expression. Those were words that doomed a romance. She was silent, but tears began flowing down her cheeks. Laura made no effort to wipe them away. He gave her his handkerchief.

I guess this is a breakup, and for such a small thing, a short separation. What had changed in so short a time?

He stood up, kissed her on her forehead, then removed a gold neck chain she had given him for his birthday and placed it in her hands before he left.

* * *

The year 1948 had proven to be a banner year for the Popular Democrats. Luis Muñoz Marín became the first Puerto Rican to be elected as governor, and his party won both houses of the island legislature. He had promised a better future; no more focusing on the status of the island, but more efforts on the economy, on jobs; that was the order of the day.

For Edwin Ferrer, this wasn't enough. He couldn't get his mind off of losing Laura, or of missing the opportunity to do something else with his life. He was trying to convince his family that he wasn't needed on the farm, that they could survive without him. He would send money home, of course, if he found a good job in New York. And he would talk to Juan, not as a brother, but as a mentor trying to help him.

He knew the choice between Laura and the big city had to be made, and he chose Manhattan, thinking he would return and find that Laura had missed him so much that she would return to him.

Edwin abandoned the idea of going to the States for only a month.

He would save the little money he had and make this trip his own personal diaspora. He would stay as long as he needed to. In one sense Laura was right; one month wouldn't change anything.

Once employed, he hoped he would return to visit his family as often as he could afford to. That made sense. He wasn't abandoning the island, but actually helping to provide for his family.

The delay left him in Sabana Grande for several more months until he could arrange a place to stay in the city up north, most likely with a cousin who had left two years ago.

Laura continued with her studies, but made her trips back to Sabana Grande less frequent. She had seen Edwin on various occasions in town and had waved to him from a distance, but they had hardly spoken. It dawned on her that he didn't leave that summer for New York after all, but since she had no close contact with him, she didn't know why that was. In her mind, a separation was a good idea, since she was rethinking her feelings for him. In that sense, time was a blessing.

Edwin actually waited almost nine months to leave, and in the summer of 1951, he boarded a plane at Isla Grande Airport in San Juan for New York. He booked passage on Pan American Flight 298, a non-stop which departed from San Juan at 11:00 at night, and arrived six hours later at New York's Idlewild Airport.

Before he left, he decided to visit Laura one last time. She was home and greeted him warmly. As they sat without speaking for a few minutes, Laura took his hand in hers. He flinched.

"I'm happy for you, Edwinsito. I know you will find a good job and be successful. You have lots of drive and ambition and want to better yourself. That is good. I'll miss you, really."

That didn't sound that very sincere to him, but he ignored it.

"Laura, I just wanted to say goodbye in person, not by mail. I know we didn't part in a good way, but that's not important. You'll always be special to me and have a place in my heart. All I want is for you to be happy, even if it's not with me." His voice broke at those last words.

"That is very kind of you, Edwin. I have good memories of our time together. But before you go, I have something to give you."

She left the porch, returned with a small white envelope, and handed it to him.

"Open it when you get home, okay?"

He stood up, they exchanged kisses on the cheek, and he left for what he thought was the last time he would ever see her.

Once home, Edwin opened the envelope, and read the note.

Edwinsito:

I know you are leaving for New York, not on vacation, but for a more permanent visit. We had fun, and I won't forget you, no matter how much time passes. Never doubt that I really had feelings for you. Here included is something of yours. Wear it not because of me, but to make sure that God be with you always.

Con mucho cariño,

Laura

The gold chain she had once given him was inside, now with a small gold cross charm attached. He put it on instantly.

Chapter 5
Boricua In NYC—1951

E dwin arrived in New York at dawn on that June summer day. He hadn't slept at all on the noisy aircraft, which was teeming with passengers and babies wailing. Once he landed and went to the baggage claim area at Idlewild Airport, he met Ruben Collado, a cousin from his mother's side of the family.

They embraced and chatted rapidly in Spanish, although Edwin was desperate to try his English on someone. He had taken some lessons from a schoolteacher in town, on his free time, and tried to practice speaking it with his family, but that didn't work.

"Edwin," Ruben said, "you are here in the greatest city in the world. *Te va encantar New York.* A lotta people, and a lotta of chances to make *dinero. Mucho dinero!*"

"Your English is perfect," Edwin said, laughing. "Is it Rubén or Ruben?"

"Whatever you want to call me, brother."

They left the airport in Ruben's car, a rundown white and green, two-door Chevy. The sun was rising at that moment, which led to a mystical glow on the skyscrapers, which Edwin had only seen in photographs.

They traveled into Manhattan and followed the East River Drive to the Lower East Side, where Ruben had rented a two-bedroom apartment with a cozy living room, a tiny bathroom, and a very small kitchen.

Once there, Ruben parked his car across from a six-story tenement building on Orchard Street. The crowded sidewalks were beginning to take shape at that hour with people heading to their workplaces in different parts of the city.

Ruben stepped out of the car and took Edwin's suitcase with him as they crossed the street to his apartment.

"I didn't expect this," Edwin said with a surprised tone.

"*Te gusta, no?*"

Edwin remained silent, and finally said, "*Sí,*" although it wasn't true.

They walked up the stairs to the third floor where Ruben lived. Inside, Edwin glanced at the interior. *Quite a mess,* he mused. *But that is typical of bachelors.*

He was led to a small bedroom with a miniature closet and a narrow single bed.

"*Primo,* this is your bedroom for as long as you want, rent free. I'm serious."

"*Gracías,* Ruben, you're a savior."

"Now really, how long do you plan to stay?"

"Until I find a job and can afford a place of my own."

"That long, huh?" Ruben laughed. "It's a joke."

"I'm confident I'll find a job in this city, better than the one I had back home. I've finished high school at night, and hope to study even more."

"What will you study?"

"Whatever will help me start my own business, here or in Puerto Rico."

"*Ambicioso, eh?*"

"*Soy muy ambicioso, créeme.*"

* * *

The interviews did not go well for Edwin. He was offered a job as a dishwasher in a restaurant, as a delivery boy for a bodega, as a messenger for a printing shop, and finally as a clerk in a hardware store. All were nearby in the *Losaida*, the Spanish nickname for the Lower East Side. He was tempted to accept the hardware job but declined, saying he wanted to think it over. But the next job interview at a garment industry workshop, with depressing working conditions, made him go back to the hardware store and accept the job offer that same day. The pay was modest, but it was a start.

Ruben was happy for him, and hopefully soon he'd have the apartment to himself once again.

"How much they gonna pay you, Edwin?"

"Not too much, but it's a clean workplace, and the owner, a Mister Vazquez, seems nice."

"How much?"

"Seventy-five cents *por hora.*"

"Wow, seventy-five cents an hour, my ....*muchacho*, you gonna get rich," Ruben said sarcastically.

* * *

Edwin was not blind—he realized the differences between living on island and working and living in New York, especially as a newly arrived Puerto Rican migrant. People here were busy with their own lives and hardly ever acknowledged his presence. The other employees at his hardware store rarely spoke to him, or would only ask where he was from, due to his accent. He would reply "from Puerto Rico," and that would end the conversation.

Ruben had warned him to not say he was from the island, but just mention that he was Spanish, to avoid being classified as an interloper. That didn't sit well with Edwin. When told that he didn't look Puerto

Rican, he at first would explain that his grandfather was from Northern Spain, then later after tiring of the questions, would answer, "What is a Puerto Rican supposed to look like?" That also stopped the chatter. He had never before experienced discrimination, and especially one based on race, but now it was different.

At night in Sabana Grande, he would be lulled to sleep by the *coquis,* the small tree frog native to the island. It was peaceful and quiet until the first crow of the rooster. In his New York apartment he heard ambulances and police sirens at all hours of the night, with cars honking their horns at three a.m. Neighbors would shout at each other regardless of the time of day, usually across the alleyways and between buildings. The noises were hard to get used to, but Edwin imagined that with time it would get easier to sleep.

One morning after a restless night, he found his roommate in the kitchen brewing coffee, using original beans from the island imported to the city by a local bodega. He gazed through a window and said, "Ruben, I meant to ask you about the funny shape of the porches here, stuck outside of the building, one on top of the other."

"Those are not porches or *balcones, bobo,* they are fire escapes, so we can get out of here in case of fire."

"Then why do so many people sit on them outside and use them for social meetings, even in the late-night hours?"

"What do you expect them to do in hot summer weather? It can reach 100 degrees here in July and August."

Later on, even though the fire escapes themselves were ugly, moldy, rust colored and dirty, Edwin got used to them, and would join Ruben, both sitting on folding chairs, to drink beer after work.

His first job in the warehouse at Jack's Hardware became a daily routine of stocking shelves. Located on the corner of 14th Street and 1st Avenue in the Lower East Side, it turned out to be a nice walk to his job in good weather, about a mile or so. In winter, it might prove challenging, he was told.

Later at the store, as he became familiar with the work required,

Edwin occasionally was assigned the cashier's job in the front, which he liked. As his English improved, he learned to answer customer questions.

The best part of his job was working alongside a young woman, Isabel Herrero, a second-generation New York born Puerto Rican of mixed race who spoke English with no accent whatsoever, but knew very little Spanish.

Isabel had lightly tanned skin, straight dark brown hair, large expressive eyes, and a fetching smile. He imagined her to be about 17 years old, but he would never ask that question. He simply smiled at her when passing or working next to her at the front of the store, or found excuses to speak to her about some merchandise or a customer.

On morning while he was on duty as the cashier, an elderly gentleman came into the store. He spoke English with an accent that Edwin didn't recognize, even though he was becoming well versed with the voices of the Lower East Side. The man bought a can of paint, a hammer, and a bag of nails and some screws. To that he added two brushes. When he went to pay for the goods, he handed Edwin a 50-dollar bill. Edwin added the prices, took the money and gave the change back to the customer. The man started walking to the exit, then turned around and asked Edwin for the missing 10 dollars. Edwin checked the receipt and looked at the man's change. He recounted and concluded that he had given the man the right amount.

The old man started arguing with Edwin, then called for the owner, Mr. Vasquez, who appeared and patiently heard him. He asked for Edwin's version. Then he opened the register, took out ten dollars and handed it to the man, who promptly left.

"Ferrer, those ten dollars will come out of your next paycheck."

"But I didn't do anything wrong, I swear."

"In this business, the customer is always right." What Vazquez didn't say was that it wasn't the first time the man had pulled that stunt in the store. As long as that man kept coming back to buy, it was a risk worth taking for the owner.

Those ten dollars that Edwin lost would affect his take home pay that week, and limit his payment of necessities, including money he owed Ruben, mostly for food and utilities. He had to accept that or quit, which he couldn't do.

He complained to Ruben, who listened quietly but said nothing. The next morning Isabel, the store clerk, approached him when they were alone and mentioned that Vazquez had done the same thing to other employees, and to her as well.

"Ferrer, just avoid doing cashier's duty as much as you can, and if that older man returns, take a bathroom break or go somewhere else."

"Why do the others accept that and not complain?"

"Do you see a union here or what?" She shook her head and walked away.

The third time Edwin had trouble at the register, he started a job search before quitting. He called in sick to cover his absence and since he had a cold, his excuse sounded genuine. Responding to flyers in the post office where he dropped off his mail most of the time, he saw an ad asking for applications to become mail delivery carriers. The pay offered seemed fair, if he could pass a test and an interview. It would be an hourly rate, paid every month, and nearly twice his present wage. It also was a steady job, with other benefits to being employed by the U.S. Post Office.

He took the test, went to the interview, waited for an answer, and he received a letter three weeks later saying he had been hired. Edwin went to the hardware store, gave his notice, and began saying his goodbyes.

Edwin met Isabel on a lunch break, told her about his new job, and asked her if they could remain friends. She gave him her telephone number and address on 28th Street and 3rd Avenue and wished him well.

Ruben was glad for him and hoped this would mean that Edwin could find a place of his own. Since Edwin would be working out of the West 38th Street and 8th Avenue post office, it seemed logical that he would move closer to his new job.

Chapter 6
The Uprisings

The year 1950 started unremarkably enough. No one suspected that in October, the Puerto Rican Nationalist Party would organize an uprising in various towns across the island, not only in Jayuya, a remote mountain town, but also in Arecibo, Utuado, Mayaguez, and finally San Juan. While the insurrection failed, it left a deep rift in the social structure of the island, which was becoming more politicized as the upcoming referendum for the adoption of a new constitution grew near. The proposed vote would also change the relationship of the island with the United States, if approved by Congress.

The political protests that had started in 1948 soon after the election of Luis Muñoz Marín as governor had gained strength, starting with the passage of the *Ley de la Mordaza* (the Gag Law), which made it crime to advocate for the independence of the island, or wear symbols of the Puerto Rican flag or even display them in public. A flag pin worn on the lapel of a business suit was technically a violation of the law. The national anthem, "*La Borinqueña*," was barred from being sung or played in public. This law was deeply resented by a large portion of the voting public, not just by those who favored independence.

Carlos Roche himself thought the statute went too far and that it interfered with the freedom of speech guaranteed by the U.S. Constitution. He anticipated that eventually it would be declared unconstitutional by the U.S. Supreme Court, but that would take years. His opinion was not shared by many in his party. The leadership wanted a unified and a solid support for Governor Muñoz, a Popular Democrat, who was the first Puerto Rican in history to be freely elected as governor.

* * *

In the family, the only dissonant voice on politics was that of Ana, Carlos's daughter, now 19, on the verge of finally graduating from high school and with plans to pursue a college education.

"Muñoz Marín is a wolf in lamb's clothing, preaching peace and island autonomy on the one hand, and betraying the island's culture and history on the other," Ana said to all who would listen.

María Antonia would let her finish, then say, "What do you propose, a revolution?"

"Something like that, but no violence."

"You are dreaming, Ana."

Muñoz Marín had once been an *independentista,* but now he said that the island's status was not an issue. For her, he was a traitor.

Ana did not believe anything that the Popular Democrats said, and as time passed, she grew more impatient with both her father and her stepmother, María Antonia, when debating partisan politics at the dinner table, always an acrimonious conversation.

María Antonia was now an English teacher at the University High School and became upset every time she heard Ana's strident comments, but withheld her opinions and remarks to preserve family unity. Her teaching job had been an advantage after Ana had been expelled from the Catholic school she attended, for pummeling another girl's face and head with her fists. The girl had said that according to her parents, all *independentistas* were communists. Due to that incident, Ana had lost nearly two years of education, refusing to go back to school. María finally got her admitted, under strict conditions, to her high school.

Carlos had punished her and placed severe restrictions on her leisure time after that suspension, but whenever Ana visited her mother in Ponce, those restrictions largely evaporated.

Ana loved the new school; no mandatory prayers, no catechism, no ugly uniforms. She felt free, and that made her happy. Carlos had noticed her change in attitude towards her studies as well, which pleased him.

"How is the University High School, Ana? Do you like it better?" he asked her.

"I don't like it, I love it. More freedom to do as I please and be myself." She smiled broadly.

"I want you to behave and restrain your impulses; you can't afford to be kicked out of school a second time. You'd never get into college, if that happened. *Entiendes?*"

"And I can dress as I please."

"Within reason," María Antonia chimed in as she passed by the living room.

* * *

Carlos was busy with managing his two business interests, but an opportunity had risen to invest in a restaurant very popular with Spanish expatriate colony in San Juan, the Casa Malatrasi, which specialized in Catalonian and Italian cuisine. The owner as well as chef, Manuel Malatrasi, who was Italian, had fallen on hard times and his health was declining. He had lost his business partner, and now was looking for investors to keep the eatery open.

Another factor was that the owner had hoped to open a small inn nearby with his profits, but he had exhausted his capital in keeping the restaurant afloat. It wasn't the right time for an expansion, but if additional investors were found, then it might be a real possibility.

He knew Carlos well, because he was the adopted son of Antonio

Roche, a dear friend. After the passing of his father, Carlos had become a frequent guest of the restaurant and Malatrasi had shared with him many stories of Italy, Spain, and Barcelona, mostly focused on cuisine.

The major problem Carlos faced was not a monetary one, but one of time. He felt that he was ignoring his family between his business interests and his political activities. Although María Antonia didn't complain, he could see it in her eyes whenever he came in late for dinner, or when he didn't show up at all. Adding a restaurant to this equation seemed foolhardy.

"Carlos, have you spoken to Ana lately?"

"Why, is there a problem?"

"What do you think? Talk to her. She won't listen to me. Remember, I'm not her mother."

"What is it now?"

"It's the new boyfriend. I fear he's a radical. A real one, I mean."

"How old is he?"

"*No sé*. But he is much older than Ana."

"Have you talked to him?"

"Many times, and believe me, he's not joking. And I say this is not because I'm a Republican."

"What is he, an *independentista*, or worse?"

"Not really sure. Definitely a radical."

"I will talk to Ana when she comes home today."

"No, you won't. She's in Ponce until Sunday night."

* * *

Ana had met Héctor Estrada, a student originally from the town of San Lorenzo, at a social gathering one evening between the high school seniors and students from various faculties at the university.

At the beginning, she barely noticed him amongst those gathered, but as he approached her, she couldn't avoid staring at the handsome student with short black hair, long sideburns, and hazel eyes, who walked as if he were in command of a squad of troops in battle.

He passed by, nodded at her, and she smiled. All of sudden he came back and introduced himself.

"*Hola.* My name is Héctor Estrada. I'm a student here in Social Studies, senior year."

"*Hola.* Ana Rodríguez. I'm from Ponce."

"What faculty are you in?"

"Still in high school, will graduate in May."

"Any idea what you want to study?"

"I think I may specialize in political science, with a minor in Puerto Rican history."

"Sounds interesting. Welcome to the campus and to our get-together. Just some advice. Be flexible in choosing a major. You will find that many of us change our minds after we have been here a year or two."

"*Gracias, fue un placer,*" she replied. They parted ways.

One afternoon days later, Ana strolled towards the exit of the campus, following the cement and stone pedestrian path which was lined on each side with tall Royal palms, extending from the entrance of the university to its famous tower. The first set of palm trees started a few feet from Ponce de Leon Avenue, at the cream-colored brick entrance gate, and ended in front of the majestic tower, which was the universal symbol of the college. The beige tower itself was decorated in the Rococo architectural style. The design was ingenious, simple and beautiful, with bas-reliefs of all the essential symbols of higher learning found in advanced education. The university had been founded in 1903, first as a teacher's college, then much later as a four-year university, and was the shining example of higher education, at its best, on the island.

Ana admired nature, and the entire landscaped grounds were populated with amapolas, hibiscus, and other tropical flowers like aleli. The campus also had a manicured front lawn, the envy of many businesses and other schools of higher learning.

She was lost in thought when she heard footsteps. Ana turned to see Héctor, who had appeared suddenly behind her. She flinched.

"Did I startle you? Didn't mean it, *perdona*."

"A little, but don't worry."

"I was wondering if we could someday meet for lunch, or a *merienda* at an off-campus cafeteria, like the one just around the corner."

"Okay, if it won't create any problems with your girlfriend."

"It won't, since I no longer have one."

"*Lo siento*, I assumed you were taken."

"I was until recently. No more."

"Didn't mean to intrude. I'll see you maybe next Friday, at noon at that café. I only have an hour for lunch."

"*Sí*."

They met the following Friday, and they mostly spoke about student life. Once she had satisfied her curiosity about the campus, she changed the subject.

"Why is there so much political activity at the UPI?" She used the slang nickname for the college.

"What are you referring to?" Héctor asked.

"Everything I read is about a student strike, a sit-in, or some other kind of protest."

"These are difficult times, believe me. Not everyone is thrilled with the government, regardless of who the governor is or which party is in power."

"My family is also divided by politics. My father loves Muñoz, but my stepmother dislikes him, not as strongly as my actual mother does. She lives In Ponce. My brother was one of the Cadets of the Republic killed in the Ponce Massacre in 1937."

"*Dios mió*. Didn't know that. You must hate the Populares."

"No, I don't. It wasn't their fault. It was the former military governor appointed by Washington, Governor Winship, who gave the actual orders to kill the cadet marchers."

"I'm not a sympathizer of the government. I belong to a student separatist group named *Estudiantes para Independencia*, or EPI. But we are not violent. We believe the people will wake up some day and claim the right to self-government, real self-government, not the 'fancy' colonial one that Muñoz wants to create." His face became red as he said this.

"When and where do they meet?"

"Why, are you interested?"

She was more interested in him than in politics, at least for now. "Yes, I am." She said it without conviction.

"Okay, I'll let you know when the next meeting occurs. Give me your phone number."

"Please don't leave a message if I'm not there. Just leave your name and phone number where I can reach you,"

"*Vale.*"

* * *

Carlos Roche awoke early in the morning of October 30, 1950 and began preparing for a normal day at the office. Later that morning, in a café close to his offices in Old San Juan, he heard a commotion while he was eating. The owner raised the volume of the radio located on a shelf behind the bar. Scattered reports were coming in from broadcast station Radio WAPA that a rebellion led by Nationalists had taken place in Arecibo, Jayuya, and Utuado. It was reported the several Nationalists had tried to enter *La Fortaleza*, the governor's mansion, in San Juan, firing bullets at the policemen stationed at the entrance with machine guns and rifles.

It was unclear at that moment how many people were involved in the multiple attacks, which by now had extended to Mayaguez and Ponce.

Carlos got up and ran to his office, then called his house to see where his family might be. María Antonia was teaching at the University High School, and Ana, he imagined, was on campus there.

Back at the office, he began a series of phone calls to his associates and friends to find out more about the attacks. Even though he had tried to forget the death of his son, Toñito, he could never forgive or forget the brainwashing that his ex-wife Margarita Rodríguez had perpetuated on the child. He remembered well the role that the extremists of the Nationalist Party had played in Toñito's death, but it was the state police and National Guard that had attacked those cadets while they marched in the doomed Sunday Palms' Day parade.

As he reached out to people on the phone, Carlos learned more details. A friend of his, who happened to be a follower of the Puerto Rican Independence Party, called him and condemned the assault. He tried to reassure Carlos that his group had nothing to do with it. Those reassurances failed to calm him.

He then called the Popular Democratic Party headquarters to find out if Governor Muñoz had been hurt. Carlos was told that the attack by the Nationalists was an attempt to assassinate the governor, but it had failed.

* * *

When Ana was apprised of the uprising, she tried to call home but no one answered, so she then called her father's office and spoke to his secretary, Alicia. She assured Ana that Carlos was fine and had been on the phone all morning calling his friends and associates of the Populares.

The next two days, local newspapers like *El Mundo* and *El Imparcial* screamed for attention, with headlines like:

Nationalists Attack Utuado, Arecibo, and San Juan
Shootout in *Barrio Obrero*
Airplanes Bomb Utuado

There also were reports on the radio of the attack on the Blair House in Washington, D.C. The *New York Times* had put the news on its front page. The article stated that Governor Muñoz had reassured President Truman that the attack was carried out by a violent extremist party. It did not represent the Puerto Rican population, nor their ideals, or affect the valued association with the United States. President Truman had responded with a sympathetic voice, and said he knew that Governor Muñoz had been a target as well.

* * *

Gabriela Díaz heard the news on the radio, then ran to her Uncle Carlos's residence on Avenida Magdalena, which was just a few blocks away from her home on Calle Caribe in the Condado district. She had moved to her own, more modest dwelling a year after her arrival in San Juan.

She was worried now about her son and daughter, both studying at the university, and guessed that if any uprising led by extremists had taken place, the campus would likely be at the center of it. The UPR was notorious for its political atmosphere, protests from both the left and the right wings of politics.

When she arrived at the Roche residence, the only person there was the housekeeper, who informed her about Carlos's absence. She had tried calling him but was unsuccessful. She had no way of traveling to the UPR to find her children, since she didn't drive and was hesitant about calling a taxi and going there alone.

As she brooded in the entrance, she heard her name called. It was Fernando, now a law student at the university. She ran and embraced him, then asked about Teresa.

"No sé, *Mamá*. The last time I saw her was this morning at breakfast. I didn't ask her specifically where she was going."

"Surely she's in class, no?"

"Not at this hour, I don't think. She took the day off and mentioned something about Old San Juan."

"Might she be at her boyfriend's house, in Santurce?"

"Let's call his parents, the Del Valles."

At the Roche residence, they rang the bell to summon the housekeeper to the front door.

"*Señora*, may we come in and use the telephone?" Gabriela asked.

"*Claro*," she replied, and led them inside.

Fernando found the Del Valles' phone number in a directory and called them, but no one answered. He then placed a call to Carlos's main office and spoke to the secretary, who informed him that Carlos was at the PPD party's central offices and it was bedlam there. She recommended that he not try to go there or even call.

Feeling frustrated, he returned home with Gabriela to plan their next move.

"I just remembered that Teresa said she was going to take the afternoon off from studies and mumbled something about going to Old San Juan. Her only class at the UPI in the morning was a final review for an exam," Fernan said.

"She never said anything to me."

"I know *Mami*, she isn't going to tell you her every move."

"So do you know exactly where?"

"No, but her favorite spot for coffee with friends is located on Calle San Sebastian, corner of Calle Cruz, the Café Vizcaya."

"Let's go get her. This is important. We don't know what will happen next."

"What was she wearing?" Fernan asked.

"A simple black blouse with a white skirt, a long one...

Oh, no, *Dios mió*, no!" Gabriela fell into his arms weeping.

"The colors of the Nationalist Party," Fernan said, with alarm in his voice.

Chapter 7
Transitions

During this time, the struggle by the local government to change the relationship of the island with the United States intensified. It reached a fever pitch when the local government presented a working paper to Congress for what would be named the Federal Relations Act, describing the new parameters of self-rule for the island.

The Nationalist revolt certainly had an impact on the perception of Puerto Ricans and its politics by the Americans. Some in Congress thought, not so privately, that if the island was not satisfied with the current state of affairs, why not grant it independence outright, even though a majority of its citizens hadn't supported that option at the polls? Insisting on a commonwealth would only bring more violence, they said.

Governor Muñoz Marín had his hands full trying to persuade the appropriate committees in Congress to take a serious look at the proposed legislation, which would first require a referendum by the island residents to accept or reject a new constitution. If the referendum vote was in favor of the change, and subsequently approved by Congress, then a law would be enacted to establish a new relationship with the American territory.

The revolt by the Nationalists certainly didn't help the cause, nor did the numerous protests against any form of commonwealth, by independence sympathizers, which had formed a political party in 1948 to participate in the electoral process. They were not of the same stripe as the Nationalists, but were hard put at times to condemn the violent actions of that group, although many members did, notwithstanding that they shared the same ideal.

To add to that scenario, the followers of the Statehood Republican Party opposed any form of commonwealth status, which they said would only delay statehood for the island.

* * *

Carlos Roche was finally informed of Teresa's disappearance by Fernan and Gabriela and of their inability to locate her. He called some of his friends in the Puerto Rican police for help, but they were too occupied with the aftermath of the uprising. In San Juan alone, five out of the six attackers died at La Fortaleza, and other bystanders had been injured by the exchange of gunfire. In the interior of the island, there had been more than 30 deaths and many wounded. The Puerto Rican National Guard had been mobilized throughout the island.

Fernan raced to Carlos' offices, where they all met and walked hurriedly towards the Café Viscaya. Upon arriving, they asked the owner if he had seen Teresa and showed him a photograph of her.

"I know the young *señorita*, she comes here often, but today she left early when she heard the commotion at La Fortaleza," the man said.

"Was she with other people?" Carlos asked.

"Yes, with another woman and a young man whom I don't know."

They left the café and proceeded on Calle del Cristo, headed downhill towards the site of the attack. Barriers had been put up by the police; they were stopped after passing the cathedral, where no further movement was possible. They were unable reach the corner of del Cristo and Calle Fortaleza, since it was blocked off.

"Carlos," Fernan said, "we can go to Calle San Jose, in back of the cathedral, to try and see if there is another path to the end of Cristo, where the chapel is."

"*Bién, vamos.*"

Gabriela, who had lagged behind, caught up with them in front of the church.

Carlos and Fernan moved slowly, looking at the guards that could be seen at the back of the church, but the policemen were not interested in them. All three moved past the rear of the cathedral and all the way down Calle San Jose.

They walked to the intersection of Calle Tetuàn, then up that street to the rear of the Cristo Chapel. There was a small pedestrian opening between the walls of the building on the corner and the side walls of the chapel. They passed through in a single file.

"There is someone lying in the gutter," Gabriela shouted as her eyes scanned the little park next to the chapel.

"Where?" Fernan said as he rushed over to her.

"Right there, it's a woman." Gabriela pointed to a body.

"Should we call the police?" Fernan said.

"I wouldn't yet," Carlos replied.

He moved forward and knelt beside the woman, placing his fingers on her neck.

"She's still alive," he said after a few seconds.

As Gabriela approached, she noticed the white skirt the woman wore, and the dark blouse, and screamed. "*Es mi nena,* Teresa!"

"What?" Carlos said.

"That's exactly the outfit she wore this morning, but something must have happened; her clothes are of similar colors to the Nationalist Party, black top and white pants. She's been wounded."

"She's been hit in the back, probably by a bullet, and she's still bleeding," Carlos cried out.

Between the three of them they carried Teresa back to the corner of Fortaleza Street, which was blocked by police. The police contingent asked Carlos if she was involved in the attack. He denied it and said she was his niece. A police sergeant recognized him from news headlines and let them pass the barricades. Later, they flagged down a motorist on a side street, and he agreed to take them to the nearest hospital.

At the public hospital in *Puerta de Tierra*, Teresa was placed on a cot in the emergency room, where she lay among several other patients. Her condition was dire, and she needed immediate surgery.

Back at his offices, Carlos made arrangements to transfer Teresa to a private hospital closer to his home, the Presbyterian Hospital in the Condado.

At the new hospital, Gabriela waited impatiently for news about her daughter. Her mind was filled with memories of leaving Barcelona in haste to save her family, and now this had happened. Her daughter had been shot in what was supposed to have been a new and safe beginning for the family.

A nurse orderly came out and told her that Teresa was being transferred to an operating room for surgery on her back. She had two fractured ribs; the bullet had grazed her spine, but missed her vital organs.

Several hours later, a doctor in a surgical gown came to the waiting room and introduced himself as he took off his mask.

"I'm Doctor Santana, the Chief of Orthopedic Surgery at this hospital."

Gabriela looked up, then wiped away her tears and stood aghast. It was the same doctor she had met and gotten to know in the voyage from Marseilles to San Juan. She hadn't seen him for almost two years, and he looked a bit older, with speckles of gray hair and some wrinkles. Yes, it was him.

They had promised to meet after their arrival in Puerto Rico, and had dinner one night at the Restaurant Zaragozana, but they had not followed up on each other. Now it was his turn to fend off surprise. He smiled at her in recognition and hugged her after discarding his gown and mask.

"This couldn't be a worse time to meet again," he said with genuine sadness. He looked down at the floor, then straight at Gabriela.

"I know. Imagine, my daughter clinging to life and you step in. I wonder if God sent you," she said.

"I feel the same. You will be happy to know that a full recovery is possible, if she follows my instructions. Two broken ribs and a spine injury can be treated successfully. She will walk with difficulty for some time, but therapy will fix that, trust me."

"*Gracias*, Pedro. *Perdón*, Doctor Santana."

"Pedro to you," he replied.

Gabriela kissed his right cheek and hugged him. They promised each other to meet again in better circumstances.

* * *

Two months after being released from the hospital, Teresa was on the mend due to her youth and that the wayward bullet had traveled straight through her body. The factures in her ribs and her spine were healing, and so was her general health.

She had been questioned at length by her mother and brother as to what had happened.

"Teresa, you almost died. What in the world were you thinking?" Gabriela asked her.

"*Mami*, I don't remember anything except that after we had breakfast, my friends and I were walking down Calle del Cristo when we heard gunshots coming from afar. We ran towards the sounds to see what was happening. Near the corner of Calle Fortaleza, I realized our mistake. We should have run away when we heard the next shots, but we didn't. I saw a gun battle taking place between men in two cars who had rifles and the police at the entrance to La Fortaleza. I tried to cross the street. When I began to cross, I felt a sharp pain in my side and started running towards the Cristo Chapel. I knew I was bleeding since my blouse was wet, but I had to leave the area. At some point I must have fainted. The rest is a blur, and then I woke up in the hospital."

"Do you know who shot you?"

"No, I didn't see anybody pointing a rifle at me. A passerby on Calle del Cristo looked at me strangely, as if I was part of the rebellion."

"That's because you were dressed in the colors of the Nationalists, black and white. Now the doctor says your days of wandering alone are over. You will need to be on crutches for some time, and you will also miss the rest of this semester at the university."

Teresa said nothing, lost in thought, but started weeping.

"What happened to your friends after you were shot?" Fernan asked.

"I really don't know."

"*Caramba*, some friends you have." Gabriela looked at her angrily. "We have to report this to the police."

Carlos, who had been listening silently to the conversation, added, "If it was a police bullet that hit her, whether intentional or not, we will probably never find out. If it was the Nationalists, the police will find out one way or the other and blame them." Teresa was puzzled and didn't understand the remark.

As time passed, the incident receded in the memory of all, except Teresa, who strangely, became a fierce opponent of independence for the island, blaming the Nationalists and others for their violent methods.

* * *

The referendum on Law 600, which would lead to subsequent federal legislation making the island a commonwealth, was handily approved by the electorate and passed by a significant vote in 1952, as did the island legislature's endorsement of a new constitution for Puerto Rico. The new "compact" included the official title for the island, *Estado Libre Asociado* (*Free Associated State or Commonwealth*), and the date of July 25, 1952 was chosen as the official date of its creation.

The usual political opposition to those events went unchanged; those who favored statehood called it a "perfumed" version of a colony, lacking in basic rights like a vote in Congress or a vote for the President of the United States, and those who favored independence said much the same thing but also called it a betrayal of a nation and its people.

Ana became Teresa's best friend after the shooting, but she was gravitating slowly towards the ideals preached by her new boyfriend, Héctor Estrada, who had become her constant companion, even with their age difference of nine years and their very different economic backgrounds.

Chapter 8
The New York Colony

E dwin started in his new job in 1953 after successfully passing the written exam of the U.S. Post Office. He was offered a position as substitute mailman, on foot, with no supporting vehicle. His initial mail routes were mostly on the West Side of the city, extending from 45th Street to the 65th Street, about 20 long blocks. It seemed to work for him. He had moved to a small one-bedroom apartment, in a dark gray tenement house, on 33rd Street and Second Ave. He could easily walk to his job, or hop a ride, and his postal route, while long and sometimes exhausting, kept him trim.

He said his goodbyes to those that he knew in *Losaida*, fully aware that he wouldn't see his friends as frequently as he had before. Ruben had asked him for a favor, if it came to pass. He needed Edwin to deliver some merchandise, on the sly, to some friends in the neighborhoods that Edwin was going to work in. Edwin didn't refuse, but realized that it might be contraband merchandise, and remained silent.

Among those that he felt would really miss him was Isabel, the clerk friend from the hardware store. He promised to visit her after he had settled down. She was living with a boyfriend in a walkup on 3rd Avenue, not too far from his own apartment.

Edwin would be alone for most of the day, since his job started at dawn with his commute to the post office station and ended well after 5:00 p.m. In a big city like New York, you could feel even lonelier than in a small town if you didn't have friends. He certainly needed them.

One day he called Isabel to see if they could meet somewhere, and she invited him to her apartment the following weekend.

On Saturday, Edwin approached the apartment building, a dark red brick structure of seven floors. Isabel lived on the second floor; her dwelling seemed ample for the size of the most residences in the city. The ground floor had a business operating as a beauty parlor.

He walked up the stairs and knocked on her door.

"*Hola* Isabel, how's it going?"

"*Hola* Edwin, come in. Let me introduce you to my boyfriend, Marcos Quijano."

"Hello Marcos, nice to meet you."

Marcos looked him in the eye and nodded. "Are you related to Ruben Collado? Isabel tells me he's your roommate."

"Yes, he is my cousin."

"He's worthless, tell him I said that."

Edwin didn't answer but wondered what Ruben had done to him.

They sat down and after an awkward silence, Isabel asked, "How do you like your new job?"

"I began a month ago, so for now it's fine. I've gotten to know the city well, that's for sure." He laughed, and so did she.

"Marcos has a good job in the garment industry and is also the super here in the building."

"Super?" Edwin asked.

"Sorry, superintendent, meaning he's responsible for caring for the entire building and having things fixed if they break down."

"That must pay well," Edwin interjected, and almost bit his tongue after saying it.

"We live rent-free, and I get a small payment out of it, but it works for us," Marcos added, not looking at Edwin.

"That must be great," Edwin replied.

"Edwin, have you met anybody interesting yet? I mean girls, of course," Isabel said.

"No, not yet."

"Well, very soon I want you to meet a good friend of mine, Paulina Negron. She is pretty, single, has a great personality. She's good people. You'll like her. She's a seamstress where Marcos works."

"Fine, let me know when and where."

They continued to chat mostly on what was happening in the hardware store. After about two hours, Edwin felt it was time to leave. He left the number of the public phone near his address so Isabel could contact him. Marcos didn't even acknowledge his departure. Edwin reminded himself to ask Ruben about Marcos.

* * *

Edwin was getting to know the neighborhoods where he delivered mail on a daily basis. Shopkeepers would say hello if they were having a good day, and sometimes bakers would give him a sample of what came out of the oven that morning. He walked into most establishments, since mailboxes were scarce, sometimes hidden by fruit crates or other obstacles. Plus, he enjoyed exchanging pleasantries with most owners. But not all of them were nice. Sometimes they looked at him as if he were an oddball, or simply ignored his presence. For the latter, he simply threw their correspondence on a counter, or if he missed, it landed on the floor. It was a neighborhood populated mostly by migrants from the island.

The post office then changed his mail route to include the neighborhoods around West 58th street stretching to the West Side highway, where he and another mail carrier at times would split both sides of 58th Street or 59th Street, from Central Park to the Hudson River. On his walks he'd curse the dog manure he stepped in, not the dogs, but the owners for their neglect.

There were signs posted on several buildings scheduled to be torn down along portions of the West Side. These would make way for new construction that would house the residences of the well to do, as well as businesses, if Edwin believed the ads.

He noticed that the Puerto Rican colony wasn't just limited to the Lower East Side, the Bronx, or East Harlem. He saw, as he walked 9th Avenue, the many bodegas, restaurants, dry cleaners, beauty parlors, barbershops, and shoe repair shops. Also present were outdoor shoeshine booths and vegetable-fruit vendors working from movable stands. These were ready to serve the massive migration from the island to the city, numbering 52,000 of his fellow citizens in one year, according to the local newspapers.

His work was repetitive and not at all challenging, which planted a seed in his mind to study at night at the City College of New York, which had an extension campus facility not too far from his home. His first choice in academic subjects was business management, but he had to take some basic courses first, among them English.

Edwin had completed high school with a GED, and passed the entrance exam to CCNY easily, having read a few manuals and spoken to friends at work on how to prepare for the test. Barely, and with little free time, he had managed to make new acquaintances and a few friends who helped him. Once accepted, he enrolled in two night courses in business.

He called Ruben to tell him the news.

"Ruben, I got accepted into college," he said excitedly. He could barely speak a full sentence.

"What? You are going to college here in New York?"

"Yes, I am. Isn't that great? We have to celebrate!"

"*Si,* come on down, we will. I also need a favor."

"*Okey,*" Edwin said, not knowing how to say no.

* * *

The invitation from Isabel, a few weeks after his first visit, was a godsend, since he had no social life.

She called him one evening, making use of the public phone at the entrance to his building, and invited him to dinner to meet a new friend. It was a setup, he realized, but he didn't mind it. His last relationship with a woman was Laura Ríos, and that had been three years ago. Edwin had tried writing a couple of times to her but gave up after his letters went unanswered.

On his way back to the main branch of the Post Office the day before, he had passed a group of young men at the corner of 10th Avenue and 38th Street who eyed him suspiciously. They were all in their late teens and looked at him and his post office uniform with derision.

"*Oye Jíbaro*," one of them shouted to him. "I have a letter for you, come and get it. It's from your *novia*." They all laughed. "If you don't have a girl, we have a woman for you, or if you need something else, we have that, too."

Edwin quickened his pace and didn't look back. Three of the men had red leather jackets with black letters emblazoned on the back— "*Los Tigres Locos.*" *What a stupid name, he thought, Crazy Tigers? A gang with that name?*

One teenager from the group started following him closely from behind, and almost grabbed his mailsack, but Edwin yanked it away, turned around and faced him down. The boy stopped, turned and skipped away after giving him the finger. Edwin looked at them for a few moments and saw there were no adults in the group. *So what they said was true. Adults never joined any Puerto Rican gangs, unlike other ethnic groups.*

That Saturday night when he arrived at Isabel's home, he knocked on the door, and she answered. Upon entering her living room he noticed two young women sitting on the couch.

Once inside, Isabel pointed to the two young women. "Edwin, this is Paulina Negron, whom I mentioned to you, and her sister, Emily. *Niñas*, this is a former coworker and a good friend, Edwin Ferrer."

Edwin smiled and said hello. He looked at Paulina, a nice-looking but plain brunette with smooth facial features and somewhat overweight. Her younger sister Emily was petite, thin, with an angelic face.

Her short black hair had a streak of silver along the left side of her head, which he imagined was bleached or dyed to remove the hair's natural color since she was too young to have gray hair. He shook hands with each, but couldn't take his eyes off Emily, who seemed shy and looked directly at him only once. Once was enough for Edwin.

Isabel offered them drinks and snacks before serving dinner The conversations started with each of them describing about how they arrived in New York and what it meant to adjust to a new culture and language. However, most of the time was spent talking about Puerto Rico, and what they missed about the island—the music, the laughter, and mostly, the magnificent beaches.

"Paulina, where do you work or study?" Edwin asked.

"At a garment factory on 23rd Street and 8th Avenue," she answered.

"And you, Emily?"

"I'm still studying part time and working in a beauty salon."

"What are you studying?"

"Education at City College. Someday I want to become a teacher."

As the conversation paused, he could tell they expected him to talk about his plans as well.

"I want to become a business owner someday. An owner of something I can be proud of. I'm tired of being a farmer, and I know that being a postman won't last forever. I would hope that the business would be located in Puerto Rico, but I'm flexible."

He was smitten by Emily, her beauty, her soft voice, and delicate manner. While he was aware that Isabel had invited him to meet Paulina, he felt no attraction to her, but felt an instant attraction to Emily.

As the evening ended, he was hesitant to approach Emily directly, so he asked both of them for their phones and addresses, then gave them his. The sisters lived in Spanish Harlem, an easy ride on the 3rd Avenue subway or the Lexington line.

He took his leave and thought about Emily all the way home.

When he reached his apartment that evening, there was a Western Union telegram waiting for him at his front door.

EDWIN—*Papi* passed away last night. Please come home.—JUAN

Edwin sat down in his apartment and pondered what to do. Unexpectedly, his father was gone. Who would be in charge of his family now? His mother wasn't healthy enough carry out the duties of head of the household by herself, and Juan might not be up to the job, even after the talking to he gave his brother. Juan's dilly-dallying with young women had not stopped. How would this affect his life now?

The next morning he made travel arrangements to return to Sabana Grande.

Part Two

Chapter 9
The Return

E dwin arrived at dawn at Isla Grande Airport in Miramar, San Juan, after a long tortuous flight from New York. The flight was overcrowded, with crying babies and the smell of carried-on cooked greasy foods that lasted all the way home.

No taxi would take him straight to Sabana Grande at six in the morning, so he hailed a *público* vehicle which, after picking up three more passengers, sped toward the town, a four-hour drive away in early morning traffic.

He felt hurled back into the past when he climbed the steps to his parents' house. His mother Monserrate was awake and making coffee, a cup of which she handed him upon his entrance. She had aged considerably during the three years he'd been away, notwithstanding the fact that she was much younger than his deceased father.

"*Mami*, how did he die? What was the cause?"

"His heart gave way, Edwinsito." He flinched at the use of his nickname, but it was her creation.

"Is that what the doctor said?" He walked to her, gave her a kiss, and hugged her tight.

"No, he said it was some other thing, which I can't pronounce."

"When is the funeral?"

"Day after tomorrow at the town cemetery."

"No Mass?"

"Just a brief ceremony at the gravesite. That's all he wanted."

"Just like *abuelo*."

"*Sí.*"

Edwin left the kitchen and went outside. Many thoughts entered his mind, among them, who would take over the coffee farm.

The funeral ceremony was brief, with the town priest giving a blessing and recalling the good things that Gregorio Ferrer had done for the town and for other people during hard times, especially during hurricanes.

The town cemetery was designed as a park at the edge of an old country road with access to Highway 1, which led north to San German and Mayaguez. Gregorio's tombstone was made of a simple light gray stone, with his name and dates of birth and death etched below those of his own father, Vicente Ferrer, the original immigrant from Cataluña via Palma de Majorca.

Edwin said a few words instead of his older brother, Juan, who was overcome with grief and couldn't speak.

"Don't be sad for *Papi. He* lived a good life and loved this island with a passion. His legacy to all of us was to be kind to one another. It's all we have to do to live a rewarding life."

In attendance was Laura Ríos, his former flame, whom he spotted among the crowd, and to his surprise, his grandfather's old friend, Carlos Roche, who had driven from San Juan just for the funeral.

After the burial, Carlos approached Edwin and asked if they could speak privately the next day in a nearby café.

Edwin agreed and moved on to greet other visitors. There was no formal reception or dinner afterwards, since that wasn't the custom at the time, but Edwin managed later to speak to Laura alone, without interruptions.

"Nice of you to come," he said to her, after a perfunctory kiss.

"I really liked your father. He always treated me like someone special," Laura said.

"That's because you are."

Edwin felt a sudden rush of emotion upon seeing her that close and couldn't help blushing a bit.

She pretended not to notice and asked him about New York. "Are the winters there really that bad?"

"Yes, they are, but you get used to it. How have you been? I wrote a couple of letters, but never got an answer."

"I know, and I'm truly sorry, but my life was complicated. I got engaged and married a fellow student at UPR, but after we wed and had a child, he volunteered to go to Korea, and was killed in action."

"I'm sorry Laura. I didn't know."

"No need, I never told you. I do have a beautiful little girl. Ángeles. Her last name is Rivera, after her father, of course."

"I'd like to meet her."

"Someday, you will."

She was moving her feet unconsciously and glancing behind him. Edwin thought she might be trying to end the conversation, so he bid her goodbye, and watched her depart the cemetery. He felt a strange sensation after she left, a sensation he had believed was gone, an attraction he had not felt for any other woman so far. *Could it be that I'm still in love with Laura after all this time, even without seeing her for so long? No, that's not possible.*

He went back to his mother at the gravesite and left with his family headed to their mountain home. They first stopped to have a light snack and coffee at his aunt's house, which was just across the road from his father's newly dug grave.

Edwin met Carlos Roche the next day at a Spanish style bakery adjoining the main plaza. He entered the eatery and noticed Carlos sitting in a far corner next to a large window from where you could see part of the plaza and the surrounding businesses.

"*Hola Carlos, cómo estás?*"

"*Bien, y tu?*"

"I was surprised to see you at the funeral."

"It was my duty. Your father and grandfather were good friends of my family, no matter the time which has passed."

"They both respected you and Don Antonio Roche, and all you did for them after Hurricane *San Felipe*. Your friendship was always a true one," Edwin said.

"It was our pleasure. And I want to make you a proposition based on the history of both our families."

"What is it?"

"My father left me some money, which I want to invest in a restaurant in Old San Juan on Calle Cruz. It was successful, but now has fallen on hard times. The owner had plans to open a small hotel next to the restaurant, but he cannot without additional capital. So I will invest what I can and under one condition, that the owner replace his manager with someone I can trust."

"What does that have to do with me?"

"I want you to become the next general manager, if you accept."

"But I know nothing about running a restaurant. I only have two years of college in business administration, and that's not nearly enough."

"I trust your capacity to learn fast, and your honesty above all."

"I have a job in New York, with the Post Office."

"Then quit and come back to Puerto Rico. Eventually you will double your income. I'm certain you will know how to revive the restaurant."

"Did someone recommend me, and if so, who?"

"Someday I will tell you, if you accept the offer."

The conversation left Edwin perplexed, and he didn't know how to respond. It was a tempting chance to do something else, wholly unexpected. *What if I fail? Yet an offer like comes only once in a lifetime. Should I leave New York behind for good? Where did the best future lie?*

He asked Carlos for time to think it over, and told him that he had to return to New York for now. Carlos agreed, but asked him not to take too long in making a decision.

On his final day in Sabana Grande, Edwin called Laura's parents' home to see if he could locate her new residence. Coincidentally, she answered the phone and agreed to a visit.

He went to the same house she had lived in during their courtship. Laura came to the porch, just like she had before their separation, and gestured for him to sit down. Edwin looked at her eyes and saw the same blue eyes he had fallen in love with. Her hair was different, combed back in the currently favored style. She looked adorable and more mature.

She smiled and asked him about the reason for his visit. He stuttered at first, then blurted out, "I'm returning to the States tomorrow and wanted to speak to you one last time."

"*Bien*," Laura said.

"Tell me about you and your husband. Where and when did he die?"

"He was wounded in Korea in the battle for Jackson Heights and was taken to a field hospital to tend to his wounds. He later died on his way to Japan, where surgery might have saved his life. His name was Lieutenant Jorge Rivera, a graduate of UPR, with a commission in the U.S. Army Infantry. Jorge was a brave man and loved me dearly."

"So sorry to hear that. I didn't even know you had married, but I suspected you wouldn't remain single for long. Where did you meet him?"

"In a class in Advanced English, a required course for me at the university. He went on to study in Natural Sciences, and I graduated with a degree in Education in just three years."

"And the daughter?"

"My little girl was born after he left. We didn't expect a baby so soon, but I now have a lasting memory of him...forever." She teared up and almost started to cry. He offered her his handkerchief and waited until she had composed herself.

"I can only imagine how you must feel. He was so young and a hero. Could I meet Ángeles?"

"She's sleeping right now. If not, of course."

A long silence took hold.

"I think I'll be going now, Laura. Just wanted to see you one last time and pay my respects for your loss."

As they walked to the steps to the porch, Laura tapped him on the shoulder. He turned around, approached and gave her a kiss on the cheek. Then she said, "Edwinsito, I regret the way we broke up. I was a child, immature and foolish, and didn't realize how much I would miss you. You left for New York, and it was over or so I guessed. I handled it poorly."

"I got over it, don't worry," he lied. "I still have your gold chain and wear it always." He turned around one last time on his way out and looked at her.

His eyes moistened driving back to his parent's home. He let the tears stream down his face. *How could he ever forget her?*

* * *

Back in New York after three weeks in Sabana Grande, Edwin faced his dilemma. Go or stay? He had almost forgotten about Emily, but decided to call her and maybe visit her.

His job had always been routine, but he was getting bored by the day in and day out of mail delivery. In good weather it was fine, as it gave him an opportunity for exercise and an energizing contact with the community. In bad weather, in the snow, ice, sleet, and assorted *mierda*, he felt like quitting.

After a few weeks went by, he wrote a letter to Carlos Roche, turning down his offer. He knew the real reason was that he was afraid to fail. If he went back and the restaurant had to close, he would be left with nothing but a bad memory. Most of all he wanted to avoid going back to run a coffee farm, the only remaining legacy of his father. He was still relatively young but wanted a secure income and stability. That is why he had chosen the Post Office.

In a letter to Carlos, he wrote,

My dear Carlos:

I have thought long and hard about the generous offer you made to me to manage Restaurant Malatrasi in Old San Juan. I was honored to receive your offer, really.

Unfortunately, I'm not ready for such a project. Maybe I lack faith in my abilities, maybe I'm afraid of the challenge. I think I could run a small business, but the one you suggest is full of risks that I cannot take right now. Maybe sometime in the near future, if it were still available, or perhaps maybe in another position with your other businesses. I'm sure working with you would be a challenge and a pleasure.

I may be making a huge mistake, I'm aware, but I am grateful you thought of me. I cannot imagine who recommended me or why, but I'm deeply honored. Hope we will remain friends even with me passing on this opportunity.

Please stay in touch.

Always, Edwin

Edwin's return to his job was not uneventful. Management at his Post Office station had changed his delivery route once more and now his immediate supervisor was a man named Bruce Collins, a second-generation Irish immigrant. He took an immediate dislike to Edwin, as he believed Puerto Ricans were stealing jobs from working class whites in the city.

On the day they first met, Collins read the rules to Edwin of what he expected of his letter carriers. At first, he found fault with Edwin's hair combed style, and then his hastily ironed shirts and wrinkled pants. Edwin didn't have anyone to do that, and he couldn't afford a laundry every day.

Collins had a large burly physique that intimidated some and bright orange red hair and freckles that you couldn't separate without a microscope. He was gruff in all aspects and didn't care whom he offended.

He started making jokes about the island, its backwardness and the constant noises in the Puerto Rican neighborhoods. He asked what skin color Edwin's girlfriend had and if any of his family members were part of a gang.

"Hey Ferrer, how is it going for you today," Collins said one day. "You're late again."

"I'm fine. Give me a break, will you?" Edwin replied.

Collins stopped for a moment.

"Are you upset with me? If you are, you know what you can do."

These exchanges went on for weeks at a time, and Edwin was afraid he would lose his temper and punch the man someday. This would mean termination at the post office, something he could not risk, plus physical harm to himself if Collins punched back.

He tried asking for a transfer to another duty station but was unsuccessful. They needed him right there, he was told. Edwin avoided Collins as much as possible and confided in other carriers as to what he should do.

A fellow employee suggested that he ignore him and not answer any jibes. Some of the other letter carriers were black, but Collins avoided speaking taunting them. There had been no real confrontation until Collins started talking about the birth rates in Puerto Rico and the fact that all Puerto Ricans must have African blood in their veins because of their skin colors. He said this within hearing distance from Edwin. When he finally said that "Spics" were ruining New York and were mutts, Edwin exploded and dropped the mail sack he was carrying. He grabbed a large cardboard box full of metal canisters, threw it at Collins, hitting him in the head and causing him to fall on his back and lie still.

Before Collins could get up and respond, several employees intervened to separate the two. Edwin brushed them off, and simply left the post office station, abandoning his duty for the day, fully aware that his job was over. *After three years, he thought. What a waste.*

A few days later, he received a call from an area supervisor saying that if he returned to work, he would be transferred to another station on the Upper East Side in Spanish Harlem. He was put on probation and could stay employed, barring another violent incident or other misconduct. Apparently, some employees of his duty station had put in a good word for him. He accepted the transfer.

An advantage of working in Spanish Harlem was that he would be close to where Emily lived with her family, and if he planned it right, he could visit her after work. Another was the fact that his route was now limited to 10 blocks. Still, he realized that his days at the Postal Service were numbered.

He had tried on many occasions to ask for a transfer, even with a cut in pay, back to the island. With his lack of seniority, this was almost impossible.

* * *

Edwin's plans to date Emily paid off. On the weekends with the subways less crammed, he was able to spend more time with her, usually on Sundays. Her sister Paulina had been disappointed that he had chosen Emily over her, but that was soon forgotten.

Emily and Edwin made a perfect couple. She loved New York, having come to the city as a child. She spoke both languages fluently—English, thanks to her education in the public schools of the city, and Spanish, thanks to her parents who spoke only that at home. She was an odd *Nuyorican*, embracing both cultures at once without dismissing the practices or customs of each one. She liked the way Americans respected time and were punctual and didn't like to wait. Speaking *Spanglish* was horrendous to her, a mix created out of slang and poorly pronounced English words. After all, she was earning a teaching degree.

At the same time, she liked informal late-night dinners with not too much planning for social gatherings, which usually erupted into dancing after the main meal was served.

The courtship was short, and when Edwin in the summer of 1955 proposed marriage, first asking her parents for permission, she gladly accepted. They were married on June 21st in a small Catholic church on the Upper East Side on 116th Street and off Second Avenue.

Instead of a reception in the traditional fashion, Edwin and Emily took their twenty guests to the Nuyorican Poet's Café in the Lower East Side to listen to music from the island, and they paid the entire bill. It truly was different and would remain a cherished memory for its uniqueness.

Their plans for a honeymoon would have to wait due to their jobs, since both of them wanted to go to Puerto Rico and find a hotel with a secluded beach where they would get to know each other better, both physically and mentally. Edwin felt that a huge void in his life had been filled. It was impossible not have feelings for Emily, who someday would be the mother of his children.

But after a year and a half of marriage, without her conceiving, they both paid a visit to a doctor. She was fertile, it was confirmed, but she had a damaged lung which hadn't been diagnosed before. The constant trouble she had breathing with a lingering cough had not been enough for her to consult a physician for a full physical exam.

The news was difficult to hear. The initial medical opinion was that she had some form of lung disease, but without more tests, it was impossible to determine what it might be. Multiple laboratory tests were made in the following weeks after the visit. The final results came in and indicated that she had contracted tuberculosis. But where and when?

"There was a woman in the beauty salon from the Caribbean who coughed constantly, and her chair was next to mine. I suppose I caught it from her, not sure," Emily said.

"How long did you work close to her?"

"About six months, then she quit."

Edwin was desperate. *What could be done to save Emily? Surgery, drugs or some other treatment?*

"*Nena*, we will get through this, believe me. Modern science has a cure for everything nowadays."

"*No te preocupes*, Edwin, I feel okay, really."

Edwin tended to all her necessities, even taking time off from his work, much of which was without pay. She started a trial of antibiotics which seemed to help, but they did not stop the progress of the disease, since there was no known cure.

It was not to be. Notwithstanding the medical treatment, and the attention of the best lung specialists that New York hospitals could offer, Emily succumbed to the disease a year later.

After she passed, Edwin met with Ruben. "What did I do to deserve this?"

"Nothing, *primo*. Shit happens. Be happy that you had her for the time you did. She was special, I could tell, even though I only met her a few times."

"My life is over." Edwin sobbed, and Ruben came over to him and hugged him.

"No, it's not."

* * *

Edwin's world came crashing down, and he even had thoughts of suicide. One thing he did do was resign from the Post Office after asking one last time for a transfer to Puerto Rico and not having it approved.

The area supervisor, Samuel Johnson, a veteran of the USPS who knew Edwin best, held on to the official resignation papers, and sought out a temporary position for him in San Juan, with less pay, to see if this would help Edwin cope. Johnson was finally successful in getting a slot for him.

Once the offer was presented, Edwin thought about it, consulted his family and Ruben, then accepted the offer but gave up his seniority in the process. San Juan was not the ideal location for him, but for now, it was much better than staying in New York. Ruben asked Edwin for one last favor related to a package he needed him to deliver along 10th Avenue, but Edwin declined once more. He suspected it was drugs.

He would return to the island and eventually find something else, knowing that a job with Carlos Roche, now in his 80s and on the verge of retirement, was probably not likely.

It was the dream of most Puerto Rican migrants of the time to someday return to Borinquen, buy a house in the countryside, and live out their days peacefully in retirement. But for Edwin, this was not the manner in which he wanted to return.

Chapter 10
The Island's Dilemma

Gabriela had been seeing Doctor Santana off and on since their encounter at the hospital, the day that Teresa was wounded in the attack by Nationalists in Old San Juan. They hadn't discussed their future. As far as she could tell, Pedro was fine with just dating after a very difficult and nasty divorce. But he had other female friends, which didn't sit well with Gabriela.

At their respective ages there was no rush to marry, notwithstanding what others might think. Each of them had grown children and were set in their ways, without wanting much drama to enter their lives. It was her hope that he would propose someday and settle down.

One night when they were in her home and had the whole house to themselves, Gabriela posed the question.

"I've had a tremendous time dating you and can think of no one else I'd rather be with."

"I feel the same, Gabriela."

"Are we going to make a commitment to each other anytime soon? Sorry to ask in this manner, but I'm not getting any younger."

"The time will come, *querida*, when I'll pose the question and we can get engaged, if that makes you happy," Pedro said, kissing her on the forehead as he was about to leave.

"*Entiendo*, I know that a true commitment is not an easy thing to rush into. I can wait if that is what you want."

"Good."

They both were socially active in the Condado Casino, the local gathering social place for families of means. Gabriela had been introduced into that world by Carlos and María Antonia Roche, but she would have preferred another environment. She felt that the people there were too superficial and fascinated only by the privilege of their status in Puerto Rican society. This coming from someone who in Barcelona once had all the benefits of a similar life.

Would the locals accept, for instance, as member of their circle, a person of a much darker skin color than theirs? No, she thought, not when they met Teresa's boyfriend, Julio Del Valle.

Gabriela realized that Julio was enchanted by Teresa, and after her recovery he had spoken about making a permanent relationship with her, since she also was totally in love with him. Julio was from a humble family in *Barrio Obrero*, with parents who had labored hard in the factories of the metropolitan area and whose grandparents had come to the island as slaves.

He met Teresa at the university cafeteria, where she had been introduced by common friends. His hair was dark, tight curly brown; his face had strong features, high cheekbones, and light brown eyes. His darker skin color was evidence of his African roots and of having traces of Taino Indian blood in his veins.

Neither Gabriela nor Teresa cared about racial distinctions, and both were proud of saying it. The island had a history of social discrimination for people of color, but not the kind of racism found in the continental United States, where racial discrimination was basically part of the culture, both north and south. Somehow on the island it was hidden but present.

"Teresa, you know that the contrast between you and Julio will have people talking, even if we both deplore that," Gabriela said to her daughter after she first met Julio.

"And who cares, *Mami*?"

"I know, *nena*, just you'll know of some obstacles you will face, if you were to marry him."

"Again, I don't care what those superficial friends of yours and María Antonia say about race. They are full of crap, *son comemierdas*."

"I agree, except that María Antonia is far from being a racist. Look what she did for the women's right to vote. Just remember that any children you might have could be *trigueños*."

"Again, I don't care. They will be *Boricuas*, a people who come in a rainbow of different colors. We are a nation of whites, blacks, mestizos, and mulattos."

* * *

Carlos Roche was in his early 80s and anxious for a way to reduce his obligations to the *Ron Borinquen* Distillery, the cement plant in Ponce, and lately, the restaurant Casa Malatrasi in San Juan. For the latter, he found an interim manager when Edwin Ferrer turned down the job, but that manager did not perform as expected, and Carlos was seeking a replacement.

His frequent trips to Ponce, Arecibo, and back to San Juan were becoming harder and harder to make. He had an assistant, but his own responsibilities were overwhelming. So when the Popular Democrats asked him to run for office as a senator in the legislature, he declined.

He considered whom he might recommend, and his thoughts turned to Fernando Díaz, his second cousin, who after becoming a citizen of the United States when he was a child, had expressed an interest in Puerto Rican politics. He was relatively young and beginning his career as a lawyer in civil matters when Carlos approached him with the idea.

"Fernando, the leaders of my party are aging, as am I, and we need new fresh blood, which can revitalize the party."

"And what role would I play? I'm not even sure I believe in your party's platform, certainly not all of it."

"I understand, but we are in a new decade. New ideas will have to be considered, and if they are good, they will be adopted, thereby improving the original platform that the party was built on. Remember, *Pan, Tierra y Libertad.*"

"People at your age don't change, nor do their politics, and I mean no offense. Muñoz Marín will never retire, and that slogan is an obsolete one that should be modernized. It sounds semi socialist."

"None taken. I'm capable of listening to the new generation of potential leaders. We are facing turbulent times and with the coming election in the States, we may have a good chance to impress the new President, especially if it turns out to be John F. Kennedy. Muñoz has already indicated that this will be his last campaign for governor and is cultivating new leaders and seeking new talent."

"I really like Kennedy," Fernando said.

"He's the future."

"Let me think about it, okay?"

"That is all I am asking."

* * *

Ana Roche became engaged to Héctor Estrada, who, having finished his studies by dropping out of a graduate program in Social Sciences and Literature, was now working in a local newspaper run by the *independentista* forces. The *Despierta Borinquen* kept a close eye on the U.S. and local governments and was quick to denounce them when it was appropriate and advantageous to their movement.

She realized that Héctor was much more radical than her, but found no problem with it, except when he was discussing with friends other, more drastic means to achieve an independent Puerto Rico.

She remembered clearly what had happened to Toñito, her brother, in the 1937 Ponce Massacre, and felt uneasy each time the subject came up of forcing the hand of the American government.

Héctor had been raised by a carpenter father and a mother who spent all her time tending to her six children and her husband. When she fell ill due to an intestinal infection, she got worse waiting for eight hours in a public hospital emergency room unattended, until it was too late to save her. The pathologist later informed the family that she had died from infected diverticulitis and peritonitis.

From this experience, Héctor's anger at the government and its mismanaged public institutions increased dramatically. He always said that in a socialist republic, that would never have happened.

His one hero had been Lolita Lebron, who in concert with others had staged an attack on Congress in March 1954. He believed her to be a true Puerto Rican patriot and admired those who emulated her.

Ana also wondered about his infrequent visits to her home and speculated that married life would be much the same with his constant absences.

"Héctor, are you sure you want to settle down to a married life. You're always on the go," she said one afternoon while he was visiting.

"Yes, of course. I love you and nothing will change that. But you were raised in a bourgeois family, and it may not let you clearly see the facts of life among the struggling lower classes."

"That's not fair. You know that I despise social attitudes and conventions, and I never go to any parties with people of the high class. They act and are different from us."

"But your mother certainly does, with her doctor boyfriend."

"Yes, she does, the same doctor boyfriend that came with Gabriela, Teresa, and Fernando from Spain when they were forced into exile, and the same doctor who saved my cousin Teresa's life."

"I didn't mean to criticize your mother or your entire family."

Héctor had conceived a plan to get close to Ana and her family to study the inner workings of a privileged life and have that serve his political agenda, but he had fallen hard for her, and this created a conflict with his motives. She was unspoiled and earnest, incapable of lying to him, being frivolous, or of having an aristocratic personality. He cherished her rebelliousness. He saw in her soul someone who was a perfect match. He would never think harming her or her family in the event of a social upheaval, which he expected would come, sooner or later.

Politics on the island had become a blood sport, with people asking first where you were born, or lived, and to which political party you belonged. It got worse when the parties adopted official colors, and even though you might have preferred to wear blue, red, or green, or yellow and white (the colors of the Christian Party), it might also mean that you were stating in a subtle manner which party you followed. Black and white colors were frowned on for obvious reasons.

It became a growing malaise, after more parties were organized and blind loyalty to them was the norm—a curse that Puerto Rico had never before endured with that intensity.

* * *

Fernando Díaz was faced with a dilemma. He loved politics, but not the way it was practiced in Puerto Rico. He understood the ups and downs of political fortunes even though he had not entered the arena.

Lies were not his way of advancing his fortunes in any endeavor, and fanaticism turned him off completely. A walk through the streets of Old San Juan was his favorite way of getting away from it all. He would finish his walks at the entrance to El Morro Castle, which was on the grounds of a U.S. Army installation named Fort Brooke. Sometimes, he would walk all the way from that entrance up to the actual fortress, crossing on a sidewalk that bordered a well-manicured lawn. At other times, he would simply turn around and walk back along Norzagary Street, all the way back to Fortress San Cristobal, the larger of the two Spanish forts. He would look down at La Perla, the poverty-stricken enclave, at the bottom of the cliff which bordered the Atlantic Ocean. He recognized how desperate and deprived the others lived, those not as fortunate as his own family.

He gave his answer to Carlos Roche, a month after they had spoken on the possibility of entering politics with the Popular Democrats.

"*Primo*, I thought carefully about your idea, and while I'm flattered, I think that this is not the right time for me. I'm just starting my law practice. I have plans to get married soon and maybe start a family within the next two to three years."

Carlos said, "I understand, Fernan. Politics is a dirty business, and you have to possess a thick skin to survive the insults, lies, and invented rumors about you and yours."

"That's one of many reasons I can't run for public office. At least, not right now."

"Remember that it's with people like you that the game can be changed for the better. Crooks and liars abound in any profession, but honest, smart, well-meaning politicians are a rarity. Don't take yourself out of the race completely. You can still do a lot of good things for your adopted land."

"I will remember that, Carlos."

Chapter 11
Broken And Renewed Ties

E dwin Ferrer returned to the island one day in January 1960 and headed to his hometown. He thought of dropping in on Carlos Roche to see about any opportunities he might still have but decided against it. He was embarrassed by the way his return to Puerto Rico had come about and wouldn't lie about it, especially not to Carlos.

He had wanted to return after having saved money to start his own business, and he also knew that he was lucky to not have been fired for striking his supervisor in New York.

Edwin called Carlos from Sabana Grande and explained that he was visiting to seek an apartment, as he had been transferred to the island. A partial lie.

"How was your sojourn in New York? Are you here to stay now?" Carlos asked.

"Yes, I think, but not sure in which town. The postal service responded to my request for a transfer to work on the island, but it's not official yet, so I took a few days off until the paperwork is approved by New York and San Juan."

"Well, once you know, please contact me. In the meantime, I would like for you to come visit and stay a few days in my home here in

Santurce in the Condado. We could visit some historical sites, also see my offices and a few other things."

"I would like to do that. Please give me a few days to sort things out and I'll call you once I'm ready to visit, but only if you don't have any other commitments."

"Good. See you soon, Edwin. My regards to your family."

The possibility of working in another venue made Edwin smile and lifted his spirits. He had the time to choose between what he was doing now and a new future, if his plans came to pass.

The Post Office had advised him that he might have to go to San Juan and begin work on a part-time basis in the mail delivery section there. No letter carrier routes were available in the surrounding towns near Sabana Grande. Full time jobs on the island were scarce.

Ana Roche had her misgivings about Héctor Estrada; he sounded more radical each time they met in groups with his friends. There was even talk about staging a symbolic strike against a weak target, like the security guard posts at the University of Puerto Rico. They would fire warning shots at the guardhouse, and then escape by car. There was no intention of killing or wounding anyone, especially a poorly paid university guard who might not even be armed.

During those conversations, Ana, who didn't like the idea or even talk of it, pointed out that someone could get hurt, whether or not it was intentional. It was a bad idea, she said more than once, but she was ignored. After that, Héctor stopped inviting her to the meetings and avoided mentioning them. She noticed and said nothing but assumed that the idea had been dropped. It hadn't.

Late on a Friday night in mid-August 1960, a group made up of Héctor and his associates, including a new friend, Armando López, drove by the lone guard post near the Track and Field Stadium at the University. After honking the car's horn to distract the guard's attention, an occupant of the vehicle fired a volley of shots at the guard post, aiming just slightly above the top of the structure.

One of the shots misfired and ricocheted off the cement wall and hit the guard, who had come running out of the guardhouse to see what was happening. The wayward bullet from the revolver struck the sentry's back, and he hit the pavement face down. The occupants in the car then sped off after realizing what they had done. The weapon had been fired by Héctor Estrada, when others became reluctant at the last minute to do so. Armando pretended to fire his gun but hadn't. Unbeknown to the rest of the group, he was an undercover policemen assigned to a terrorist task force of the Commonwealth Police Department. His mission was to infiltrate separatist groups and report their activities to his commander, Lieutenant Néstor Espinosa.

The next morning, all the island's newspapers broke the news—"

Shots fired at guardhouse at UPR. Wounded guard in serious condition. Brown car fled the scene. Police are investigating."

Ana saw the San Juan Clarion's front page and confronted Héctor.

"So you people went ahead and did it anyway? You should be proud of almost killing the poor *diablo*."

"We didn't mean to do it, it was a mistake," Héctor replied, embarrassed.

"Hell of a mistake. He could die. Do you even know his name? Well it's Luis Montalvo, he's at the University Hospital, and no one knows if he will survive."

"I'm sure he will be okay. He's young, isn't he?"

"According to the paper he's 26 and married with three children, who may soon be without a father. They are a humble family from the slum of *El Fanguito*. Is that your path to social revolution and independence for the island?"

"As I said, no one intended to harm him."

"You are all cowards, shooting at a poor unarmed *guardia de palito*."

Later that evening, Ana started packing the personal things which she kept in his apartment, where occasionally she spent the night. All this, after lying to her father repeatedly about her whereabouts.

She told Héctor that she needed to be away from him for a time. He knew it was useless to stop her. She was headstrong and did as she pleased, which was a trait he usually admired in her, but now it was damaging their relationship.

"When will you return?" he asked.

"When I'm ready. Just hope and pray that the man you shot survives. It was you who shot him, right?"

Héctor said nothing and turned away as she left.

News reports in the following weeks stated that even though the university guard had survived the attack, he would be paralyzed from the waist down, and that it was doubtful that he would ever walk again. That meant he was permanently disabled and could not return to his job.

When Ana read the latest reports, she decided to break up with Héctor to protect herself and her family from unwanted publicity and shame. One death in the family due to political reasons was enough.

María Antonia and Carlos asked about the reasons for the breakup when they noticed that Ana had stopped seeing Héctor, but she invented an excuse and provided no details.

* * *

Héctor showed up at the Magdalena mansion a few weeks later and asked for Ana. She came to the door, but did not invite him in.

"Ana, have you left me for real, or is this just a brief separation?"

"I don't know yet, but if you continue doing the things you just did, we are finished."

"You want me to change my politics? I can't do that."

"No, I want you to quit that group of fanatics you joined and reject all forms of violence. If you do, then maybe, just maybe, we can talk about a reconciliation."

"I'll see what I can do, but no promises."

"You have a choice. It's them or me. I'm fed up with all this violence."

Ana said goodbye and slammed the door before he could respond. She didn't tell him about her recent medical examination.

* * *

A few months later, Edwin arranged dates for an overnight visit with Carlos at his home in the Condado. He would stay one night, he surmised, but the actual visit might probably last the entire weekend. He hoped his gray rusty seven-year-old, two-door Studebaker, which he had bought earlier, would make the trip over the mountain roads to San Juan.

After he arrived at the Roche residence and unpacked, the two went to Old San Juan and ended up at Casa Malatrasi, where they had a late lunch and were attended by the owner himself. The interior of the eatery was decorated in the classic Spanish old style, with red and black velvet covered walls, posters of bull fights of yesteryear in Madrid, rusty swords with shields, and an occasional display of actual bull horns. Music of the bullfights was on a recording but was limited in variety and repeated endlessly.

The tables were made of brown maple wood, with black leather and dark maple armchairs that matched the tables perfectly. There was a small lamp on each table with faux candles, accompanied by an ashtray of rust colored iron. This touch, with two large white plates and silverware, completed the table setting.

"Carlos, thank you for the lunch," Edwin said after they had finished eating and were sipping coffee.

"It is my pleasure, Edwin, and I hope you will return and keep visiting us. Do you like this place?"

"I do, but frankly the decor needs some updating. The menu is fine, but it could use some changes as well. This is the New World, after all. And change the music."

"Glad to hear you say that. I was hoping for some advice from a person who hadn't been here yet."

"Did you hire a new manager, and if so, how is that working out?" Edwin added.

"I'm part owner now, and with Señor Malatrasi's approval, we had to let several candidates go."

"Sorry to hear that," Edwin said as a courtesy.

"The job is still yours, if you want it."

Edwin was stunned and did little to hide it. He swallowed hard.

"Can I have some time to think about it, after I return to Sabana Grande? I'm supposed to work with the Post Office for a certain amount of time, as a condition of the transfer to the island."

"*Claro*, take all the time you need, but come back, *okey*"? Carlos grinned broadly as he noticed the sheepish look on Edwin's face.

Edwin was elated that the trip to San Juan had been so successful in such a short time after his return to the island. Back home, he consulted with this family on what to do.

Juan, his oldest brother, told him that the restaurant business was a risky one; he might lose his shirt, and a steady salary from the U.S. Post Office would provide him with a good stable career and retirement.

His other siblings, Daniel and Christina, offered different opinions, but both agreed that such a business would be exciting and challenging, and the eatery could eventually lead to good money.

Monserrate told him to do whatever would make him happy. She also informed Edwin that Laura had visited a few days ago and asked about him. She wanted to see him.

Edwin could hardly believe it—two pieces of good news in such a short time. *Might this be a prelude to a rebirth of his romance with Laura?*

He received a telegram the next day, stating that he should report to work on July 1, 1960. He had been assigned to the Mailing Division of the central post office in Old San Juan on Calle Recinto Sur.

It was welcome news for Edwin. This would facilitate his decision to change occupations if and when the time was right.

* * *

María Antonia hadn't spoken to Ana for a week or so, since Ana had gone to Ponce to visit her mother after her breakup with Héctor Estrada. She noticed Ana morose upon her return and waited for a moment when they could speak privately and without interruption.

She was Ana's stepmother, after all, and she thought it might be a time to gain her confidence, if not complete trust.

Her job was now a college professor, having been selected by the university to teach American History 101. María Antonia would have preferred another subject but knew that the Governing Council of Higher Education would never approve her teaching Puerto Rican history due to her political leanings. But she had more experience than ever before in handling young adults, since they came from all levels of society with varied backgrounds. Sons and daughters of sugarcane workers studied next to the descendants of doctors, lawyers, scientists, and other professionals.

She attempted to open a dialogue with her stepdaughter. "Ana, I have noticed that you are not yourself lately. Is something bothering you?"

"No, it's nothing."

"Please speak to me. I'm not a stranger, and I'm not your father."

"It's a matter of love lost, so you wouldn't know."

"You really believe that? Don't you recall the history of your father and I when we met?"

"Just a few bits, that's all. You were the reason for his divorce from my mother, weren't you?"

"I was not, and you know that," María Antonia said. She became emotional and tears started welling up.

"I'm sorry, I didn't mean to hurt you. It's that I'm going through a difficult time right now."

"I can tell. That is why I want you to speak to me from your heart. Just say what's on your mind, that's all. I promise I won't judge you and it will be our secret."

Ana told María Antonia all that had happened between Héctor and her, including the suspicion that it was he who had fired the shots at the university guardhouse that wounded the watchman.

María Antonia was stunned but held her tongue until Ana had finished. "Is it over between the two of you?"

"I think so, but there is something else, María."

"What is it?"

"I'm pregnant, and if Father finds out, he will disinherit me. Please don't tell him. I haven't even told Héctor, the father."

"Both of them have the right to know, and you won't be able to hide your condition for long. It should be you that tells them."

She went over to Ana, and for the first time ever, hugged and kissed her forehead.

* * *

As the weeks passed and Ana began to show, notwithstanding her attempts at hiding her belly with loose fitting blouses, skirts, and dresses, it was time to tell the truth.

She arranged a meeting with Héctor at the cafeteria where they had first had lunch. He arrived and after a few moments she said, "

I have something to tell you."

"What is it? Are you coming back?"

"I love you, but I don't know if I can live with you and your real passion, the political arena."

"You said that before, I know."

"But something else is now in the mix. You are going to be a father in a few months."

Héctor swallowed hard and felt lightheaded. "*Que?* When did you find out?"

"Several weeks ago. I'm due in the spring."

He reacted badly. "Aren't you going to get rid of it? We can't start a family right now!"

"I love your words of support."

"I'm not trying to be difficult, it's just that I don't want to settle down."

"I just thought I should tell you. Do what you want, but I'm going to have this baby, and not give it up in adoption. I can do it alone."

"Don't you even want to come back to me?"

"No, I just want you to recognize the baby when it's born, so I can eventually tell the child who you are. I don't even care if you help support the baby or not."

"I see."

Ana rose from the table. "It's going to be a girl." She then walked out quickly without looking back.

* * *

One evening at home, a month after her conversation with Héctor, Ana approached Carlos while he was reading the local newspaper and asked to speak. María Antonia was not present.

"*Papi*, I want to tell you something," she said.

"*Que es?* Are you going to get married?"

"No. I'm pregnant. And I don't want to marry Héctor Estrada, who happens to be the father."

Carlos dropped the newspaper, then stood and glared at Ana. "Say what?"

"I will not marry a man who prizes politics more than he cares for me."

"And what will you do with the child when it's born?"

"I will keep it. I don't believe in abortion, and there won't be any adoption. I want to raise the child myself."

"Who else knows this?"

Ana resisted telling him that she had confided in María Antonia first, but felt obliged to do so, even if it meant a flareup between her father and María.

"Only María Antonia. And of course, Héctor."

"What did he say when you told him?"

"He didn't take it well. But I asked him to recognize the child."

"He had better, if he knows what's good for him"

Carlos sat down to think about what he had just learned, but would never consider disowning Ana, or punishing her in any manner. On the contrary, she needed him now more than ever.

"Will you tell Margarita, your mom?"

"In due time."

"Alright. All I ask is that we keep it that way," he said.

Chapter 12
Love, Peace, And Politics

E dwin moved to San Juan to live during the week and start his job working at the main post office. He spent the weekends in his hometown, but the travel every single week was grueling. After a few months, he decided to move permanently to the city. He contacted Carlos Roche and accepted his offer to manage the restaurant in Old San Juan, but only under two conditions.

He would report to the owner on a day-to-day basis, but given the fact that Carlos was the one who hired him and owned a majority of shares in the business, only Carlos could fire him. Also, he wouldn't start full time until he completed his verbal contract with the post office, which tied him to the job for at least six more months. In the meantime, he could work part time in the eatery after he finished his day job. Once the six months had passed, he would resign as a postal worker and start full time work.

Carlos, after informing the owner, Malatrasi, and getting his approval, accepted the conditions.

The week to move to San Juan came, and Edwin wanted to let Laura know. He had visited her often, but not with enough time to reestablish his relationship with her.

"Laura, I have some news for you."

"You first, Edwinsito, because I have something to say as well."

He cringed at his nickname that she still insisted on using. "I will be moving to San Juan next week. The commute is too hard for me to work in the post office there while living here. But later, I plan to work full time in the restaurant business."

"What will you do in a restaurant?"

"I'm going to be the general manager of a well-known Spanish meson, and maybe later help establish and manage an adjoining inn."

"Nice title, but you will still be working for someone else, no?"

"Yes, at first. But later I may buy a share of that establishment or one similar. I haven't given up my dreams of owning my own business."

"I'm glad to hear that, but have you thought about the fact that places like that open and close all the time?"

"I'm aware, but I have savings and can withstand a blow like that, if it happens."

"You have courage, *cariño*," she replied.

"I'm sure you don't want to talk just about me, so let me know what's on your mind."

They moved to the living room after their exchange on the porch, and both sat down. She wore a light violet dress, and with her hair tied in a ponytail, she was the perfect image of a doll with her flawless makeup.

Edwin stared at her, then suddenly realized it was rude, so he asked about her situation and her daughter.

"Ángeles is fine. What I wanted to tell you last time, but it wasn't certain, is that I'm leaving Sabana Grande and moving to Hato Rey, a suburb in San Juan. I took a job at the Teacher's Hospital there."

"When?"

"Next month, once I finish some personal things here."

"Do you know where you will live?"

"At the beginning, with relatives close to the hospital. I will work there as a liaison for poor families."

"You mean like a social worker?"

"Very similar. I had hoped to teach someday, but this is a good opportunity for growth."

"Will you stay in touch?"

"Of course. Why do you think I asked see you?" She grinned as she said this, with a twinkle in her eye.

"As will I, since we won't be far from each other.

Edwin felt the blood rising in his cheeks, not sure why. He stood up and kissed her, not on the cheek, but a quick kiss on the mouth, which she returned hesitantly. His dream of reuniting with her might happen after all.

* * *

María Antonia had delved in politics all of her adult life and had been instrumental in the late 1930s in getting the local legislature to pass a bill granting women the right to vote. Now older, she had the credentials and was highly respected by her political group. But lately, the conservative wing of her party, closely affiliated with the National Republican Party, had decided that under no circumstances would they cooperate with the Popular Democrats to pass laws that might help alleviate the overpopulation problem and the accompanying poverty it had created. This she found unreasonable.

She was flabbergasted that even the most meritorious ideas to help the economy recover were rejected due the origin of the same, not due to their merits. She, and many more of her fellow statehooders, were growing impatient with the ruling elders of the Statehood Republican Party, especially after a 1967 island wide plebiscite showed a rising interest in the statehood ideal. The elders kept on using the same refrains from past political campaigns, which meant nothing to younger voters. Even though statehood, as a choice of the electorate, did not win the majority vote in the referendum, a splinter group, which had also pushed for statehood, formed another political entity and adopted the same referendum symbol they had used on the ballot, naming the party the New Palm Party.

They would collect signatures to participate in the next general election under the new symbol and name and form a party, which they hoped would someday result in electing a new legislature and possibly a new governor. The sky was the limit. The first step was to use young men and women to foster its ideals. A new beginning for Puerto Rico was the goal.

María Antonia was inspired by its leader, Luis A. Ferrè, a philanthropist and millionaire. She was also among the oldest women on the governing board and realized she had to make way for future generations.

She asked Teresa to sit with her one morning while she had breakfast with Gabriela at her Magdalena Avenue house. After coffee was served, she asked Teresa what, if anything, she had learned about politics on the island, especially after her encounter with the Nationalist revolt.

"I've tried to forget that chapter of my life, María."

"I will bet you haven't forgotten."

"I'm still trying, but it's not easy."

"I know. Do you have any feelings or ideals about the future of this island?"

"Of course. This is my home now. I feel like a *Boricua* inside and out.

"Are you willing to share your thoughts with me?"

At this point Gabriela, also present, was clearly uncomfortable with the tenor of the conversation and asked, "Do we have to do this now?"

"It is fine, *Mami*, I can answer. María Antonia, I don't believe in independence for the island. It would ruin us economically and cause more political instability. Also, I'm not sure if the present situation as a Commonwealth really is the solution, or if it's just a path to a friendly separation from the U.S."

"What are your feelings about statehood for the island?"

"It's complicated. It may bring more economic security, and social benefits, but at what cost? Language, culture, and customs are surely going to be affected. But my main concern is how can we obtain statehood from a Congress that doesn't want us, if you can judge by their lack of actions? This is 1968, not 1898."

"I realize that it's a perception, and it has aspects of racism tied to it. The Americans are still struggling with that issue, if you read the news from the mainland," María Antonia said.

"I do, and it has caused civil unrest there. So, if we were admitted as a state, would we be treated as equals, no matter our language, culture, and the color of our skins?"

"I would think so."

"I'm not so sure," Teresa replied. "I know that racism exists here also, but it is not as institutionalized as it is in the U.S. Would Congress want a mixed-race poverty-stricken island as a state?"

María Antonia didn't answer.

* * *

Edwin took over full time operations as the general manager of Casa Malatrasi as promised, after his temporary appointment with the Post Office expired. He said his goodbyes and sent a short note of appreciation to Samuel Johnson, the man who had facilitated his transfer to Puerto Rico.

Once situated, he put together a new organizational chart and a reporting line directly to him of all the employees. In the process, he realized that he was short of staff. He needed a sous chef, a waiter, and a line cook, the latter specializing in desserts.

He sent out feelers to other establishments to see if any of their employees needed to find another job due to the slump in the restaurant business. He also placed an ad in a local newspaper, which produced a few responses but still left him one waiter short.

Surprisingly, one person who knocked on his door was Ruben Collado, with whom he had lost contact for the past year.

"Ruben, what are you doing here?"

"I was visiting my family, whom I hadn't seen in a long time, and saw your ad in the newspaper. I wasn't aware you had changed jobs and moved to San Juan."

"It's a long story. Please come in and sit."

Edwin ordered coffee and pastries from the kitchen, since it was too early for lunch, and he had many duties that day.

After catching up on each other's latest events, Ruben finally asked him about a possible place in the business.

"Are you telling me that you are looking for a job?"

"In fact, I was wondering if you had something that I could help out with."

"Are you staying on the island? What about your job in New York and your apartment?"

"I gave up the rental and packed my belongings. I quit my job."

"What happened to make you take such a drastic step?"

"Well, I had my own little business, which supplied extra income since my day job was dull and paid slave wages, but it failed."

"And what else?" Edwin could tell that something had happened to Ruben, and now it was time to help him.

His cousin hesitated, then said, "I fell in deep with a group that wanted to expand their drug business through me. At first, it was only small bags of marijuana, and that caused me no problems. Then later they wanted larger packages to flow through me, and I suspected it wasn't just marijuana. Do you remember that I asked you twice to deliver a package for me and you declined? It was the best decision you ever made. That was the business."

"Yes, I remember even after I lost my wife. I recall that it upset you as it did me."

"Well, they came after me when I said *basta* and threatened to report me to the police through an undercover cop who had infiltrated the gang. I have left New York, but that doesn't mean they will give up looking for me, and I can't stay with relatives forever. I'm here now and need a job. Anything, Edwin, anything."

The plea was hard to ignore. Edwin could hear him loud and clear.

He could not refuse Ruben, his cousin, after all he had done for him in the Lower East Side when he first arrived in New York.

"Could you work as a waiter? It's a hard and thankless job, and your tips will easily be a large part of your real salary. You just don't seem the waiter type to me."

"I'm aware that it will take some adjusting. But I'm desperate now, and something better will appear, I know. And I would never quit on you, without lots of notice," Ruben said.

"Would that include staying on the job until I can hire a replacement for you, if you decide to leave? Most employees give little or no notice."

"I understand, and I will. You have my word, Edwin, *mi hermano*."

"Okay, it's a deal. When can you start?"

* * *

Ana gave birth to a little girl named Carmencita, and was surprised that Héctor came to visit her a month later and legally recognized the child as his. He was added as the father on the birth certificate. It was a welcome gesture, but it didn't signify that they would reconcile. For Ana, that was all she wanted.

Carlos and María Antonia welcomed the new baby, and even though María Antonia had given up hopes of being a mother herself, she embraced the role of step-grandmother with joy. The new girl would be known as Carmencita Estrada Díaz.

Héctor, as the father, didn't know exactly what role he would play in the child's upbringing, but he assumed that Ana would define it for him. He was heavily involved with his separatist group and felt that not living with Ana and their child was better for all of them.

Ana was working as a substitute teacher at a local Catholic elementary school, as luck would have it, which paid bottom level wages since it was a private school. Carlos hired a nanny to take care of his granddaughter and played with Carmencita frequently. Ana and

Carmencita were lodged in the separate guest house that had been used by Gabriela and her children when they arrived from Barcelona.

* * *

Carlos was heavily engaged in the political skirmishes that had erupted since Luis Muñoz Marín had kept his promise not to run again for governor, instead choosing his Secretary of State as the candidate in the elections of 1964.

Roberto Sanchez Vilella had won that election for the Popular Democrats with little trouble, but the voters were tiring of the 24-year reign of local politics by that party. There seemed to be a feeling in the air that it was time for something new and different.

When the followers of statehood made a strong showing in the results of the plebiscite for the status of Puerto Rico in 1967, it led to formation of the New Palm Party.

Teresa thought over carefully the invitation of María Antonia to join the woman's group of a new political party and be part of a fight for a change, real change, not just campaign slogans about women's rights and other issues plaguing the island, like the rise in crime and drug traffic.

She informed María of her decision, and since she was not working at a full-time job, she could put her efforts into registering voters and the new party.

Gabriela had her reservations, but Teresa was now an adult with a college education and could make her own decisions, like the one she was about to make in marrying Julio del Valle. Gabriela did not know this yet.

* * *

Governor Sanchez Vilella charted his own pollical path through the four years of his tenure, and due to his personal political choices and a divorce, he fell out of favor with the party elders who controlled the Popular Democrats' organization. He was not endorsed for another term as the candidate for governor of his party. Given this reality, he broke away from the party and founded his own political movement named the People's Party. He took its helm to run again as Chief Executive in 1968.

He ran a strong campaign and attracted young professionals such as Fernando Díaz, who was now a known attorney in private practice, specializing in civil law.

It wasn't enough. The tide of public sentiment was with the New Palm Party and its leader. The People's Party split the vote of those who backed an autonomous relationship with the United States, and it led to slim victory of the New Palm Party over its main rival, the Popular Democrats. A first in island history.

María Antonia couldn't believe her eyes when viewing the results late that election night. Teresa joined her in celebration, caught up in the moment, but soon realized that the work of modernizing politics and reforming government in Puerto Rico was just beginning. It was a real modern two-party electoral system for the first time in island history. The new organization had its work cut out for them.

"Can you believe this?" María Antonia shouted, jumping up and down when she heard the news from the Board of Elections.

"It really is a new beginning for Puerto Rico," Teresa said.

"So much to do in so little time. We must celebrate this event."

"*Arriba la Palma!*" Teresa said as she screamed.

* * *

Gabriela noticed how thrilled María Antonia became, and saw that Teresa was less restrained in her joy.

The sadness in Carlos Roche's face said everything. Not stopping to think, she blurted out, "Politics will ruin this land, as it did in Spain. It's a deadly sport; winning means everything, and no one stops cheering until there is blood. It is much like a bull fight, except the bull there dies quickly and with honor, after which comes the applause of the bloodthirsty crowd."

They all turned around and looked at her in disbelief. She had never spoken a word about Puerto Rican politics. They didn't know that Gabriela had just given Pedro Santana his marching orders after she found out that he was involved with a nurse at the hospital where he worked, a nurse who had become pregnant. She feared that the rest of her life she would live and die alone, like the bull in a fight.

Chapter 13
Decisions

Héctor Estrada had been raised in a *caserío, slang for* a housing project for low-income people. He had never lived in a separate dwelling from his family, always with his parents and eight siblings, never enough room for him to have any privacy. He had felt alone nevertheless, and he struggled in high school but managed to receive passing grades, with a natural knack for doing well on standardized tests. His mental retreat was his collection of books about baseball.

Due to his good scores on the entrance exam to the University of Puerto Rico, he was admitted to the General Studies program as a freshman, assigned to a section for students who showed promise but who had applied late to enter the university or who came from disadvantaged backgrounds and couldn't afford the entire tuition. He was the first person in his family, going back several generations, to go to college.

Héctor, a natural rebel, was quickly drawn to circles of students that protested life on campus, island politics, and injustices real or imagined. Most of all he was drawn to groups which challenged the system, be it the educational one or the government.

Working part time at a local bookstore in Old San Juan, he

managed to save money for a jalopy, which made his trips to and from the Isla Verde, the Llorens Torres projects, more bearable. New friends were struck by his good looks, his height, and the fact that he did not resemble or act like someone raised in public housing. He made an effort to wear freshly washed and pressed clothing with shiny shoes. His conversations were always very polite, not like some of his class-mates, who used foul language constantly and often derided female students who ignored them. His appearance was faultless, with a care-fully trimmed mustache and extra-long sideburns.

Héctor wasn't able to finish his degree in Social Studies in the customary four years. He enjoyed campus life too much, since it was an escape from his home. He found no problem in not carrying a full load of credits in his senior year, thereby extending his student status for another semester or two.

Tuition was affordable, less than 64 dollars per semester, so it presented little economic challenge. After his first year, he obtained the distinction of being an Honor Student, thus being exempted from paying any tuition. Even though he lost that privilege for not carrying a full load in his senior year, he didn't mind. That was when he met Ana Roche, and by then he was already part of the student organization Students for Independence (EPI).

As he looked back on those days, he was torn between the guilt of not having dedicated more time to his studies and to Ana, and too much time to student extracurricular activities, mainly his separatist friends, activities not sanctioned by the college.

When Ana left him after the campus guardhouse incident, he vowed to never again become involved in what could result in injuries to innocent civilians, but much later found excuses to plan strikes and create categories of persons, like policemen, that he wouldn't mind hurting. It was an alley without an exit, as was often said in Puerto Rico.

After learning of Ana's pregnancy, he vowed to extricate himself from his circle of separatist friends, but found it hard to do, being in a quasi-leadership position. He couldn't help but get excited at planning marches, setting up picket lines, and occasionally disrupting normal campus life. It was like a drug, a stimulant.

Once his daughter was born, he promised to not disappear from Carmencita's life; she was the child he had never wanted or planned for, but one now loved and accepted. It didn't matter whether he was married to Ana or not.

However, matters were getting complicated at the EPI, and the members wanted to create a symbolic but significant disruption of Puerto Rican life. The plan they worked on was to blow up a substation of the government electric energy company in Monacillos, outside Rio Piedras, near a residential suburb on Highway 1. They failed to obtain the necessary explosives that would damage it significantly, so they settled on Molotov cocktails.

They approached the substation in the wee hours of the morning of January 5th, the eve of Three Kings' Day, a national holiday, and threw six Molotovs at the steel structure. They sped away in a car, not witnessing the damage. As it turned out, the gasoline in the bottles did explode, but caused only minimal destruction. The main power grid to the substation was cut off for a few hours, but a backup system restored the energy soon. It was a typical blackout for portions of the metro area, but it was nothing unusual and was ignored by most.

The plan had failed; the group had to hatch another one.

* * *

Ruben Collado wasn't totally honest with Edwin about the reasons for his abrupt departure from New York. Sure, he loved the hustle and bustle of the metro area, with unlimited opportunities for work and, of course, diversion. But his marijuana habit had gotten him involved with some shady characters in the Latino community. If that wasn't enough, the treatment he received at his part-time job at a garment manufacturing company was humiliating. He had to escape somehow, thus the drug habit found a dedicated smoker.

His fellow workers, who were not Hispanic, often made caustic comments to each other about the Puerto Rican explosion in migration to the States, using as examples the welfare rolls in the city that had become inundated with Puerto Rican families seeking economic relief. The *barrio* was now officially known as Spanish Harlem, and that is where Ruben met his drug suppliers. After a few months, they asked if he would sell small bags of marijuana for a commission in his own neighborhood. He agreed.

As he circulated among his neighbors seeking buyers, the sons and daughters of his friends would sometimes tell him, when he asked about how they were doing in school, that they felt like foreigners in New York, and those children in middle school told him that when they returned to the island during school vacations, they felt like outsiders.

Aliens in two lands, he thought. He knew the feeling well, since he had lived through that experience. A man without a country.

Ruben heard from younger kids how hard it was to learn English upon arrival in New York, and that they could barely understand the teacher. Some children had been sent to schools for "retarded" children because of their inability to speak English.

Ruben had read about the fact that English wasn't widely taught in the island's public schools after 1949. He felt conflicted by listening to the parents and children and at the same time trying to sell his illegal product to his neighbors.

According to the newspapers he read later in San Juan, the education authorities in New York City had finally put an end to the practice of treating the Hispanic school age children as learning impaired, once the practice became widely publicized and a polarizing political issue.

He realized that the day would come when he would have to quit the marijuana business and it would be very soon. He began planning his exit from the city.

Ruben was happy that Edwin had given him a job, but he knew that he would be tracked down by his gang associates and made to pay for a missing shipment of drugs that had been assigned to him.

At first, he told the gang members he had to leave New York for a family emergency, and they had agreed to forget the lost drugs with the condition that he explore the market for distribution of a new product in San Juan. They provided him with another package which he did not open. As he started packing, he hid the drugs in his suitcase, in a secret compartment that only he knew how to access. His luggage had passed through the New York and San Juan airports easily.

As he began work for Edwin, he bid his time to figure out an exit from his situation.

"Ruben, it's nice to have someone here that I know and can trust," Edwin told him when he reported to work the first day.

"Glad to be here, Edwin, or boss, should I say?"

"Your excellency would be alright," Edwin replied in jest.

"I look forward to helping you make this work. You have lots of competition here in the capital."

"That's true, I know."

"Also, Edwin, I need a favor."

"Of course. What is it?"

"I have an inheritance matter which I didn't finish here before I left for New York years ago. I'm going to need an attorney. Could you help me find one?" It was a veiled reference to his precarious state.

"I'll ask Carlos Roche, part owner and family friend, if he can recommend a good one."

"*Gracias.*"

* * *

Edwin finally found time to visit Laura in Hato Rey at her relatives' home in Baldrich, a residential area near the hospital where Laura was employed.

They had not seen each other for several weeks, their jobs consuming most of their time during the week, and Edwin was particularly busy on the weekends.

By now Ángeles, Laura's daughter, was about to enter kindergarten and was at the ideal age for Edwin to win her over during his renewed courtship of Laura. Like her mother, she had light hazel-colored eyes, and dark blond hair, which when braided also made her look like a little doll. Her laughter was loud, and it would soon turn into a giggle when he made funny faces at her.

Edwin was unsure at what point the relationship with Laura would turn into a serious romantic one.

"Laura, do you think you could join me for dinner during the week? It's hard for me on weekend nights."

"If you give me some notice, I'll hire a babysitter, since I don't want to bother my aunt and uncle. They are older, and it wouldn't be fair to have them look after Ángeles."

"How about next week? I'll take you to a nice new restaurant in Old San Juan, not the one I work in."

"I wouldn't mind visiting Casa Malatrasi."

"I don't think I want my employees to exaggerate their efforts just to please me. This is a private dinner and I know just the place."

"When would you like to go?"

"Is next Thursday okay with you?"

"That's fine."

This real date with his first love became the first of many, and Edwin was in heaven. Laura was still the woman he had fallen for all those years ago and she hadn't changed, except in one way—she was more mature and certain of herself. But an unknown factor was if she still had feelings for him.

He looked at her with an inquiring look at times but said nothing.

She recognized that gaze. She glanced down at her food and smiled.

* * *

Teresa Díaz and Julio del Valle were on the verge of getting engaged. He had a good job at a company specializing in providing accounting services to the San Juan business community; she was still employed by the Catholic school, now fulltime. The income of both was enough for them to think about marriage, but first Teresa wanted to introduce him to her friends and the rest of her family who hadn't met him.

She had resisted her mother's suggestions that they go to the frequent social events at the Condado Casino, and she feared that Julio might react badly to any racial overtones that he might encounter there. The racial prejudice was subtle, not overt. Some members of the Casino, she imagined, would shake hands with him and smile, while others would avoid contact and wave from afar, but nothing offensive would ever be spoken.

She finally accepted an invitation from María Antonia herself, who was active in the Casino planning committee for special events, like *quinceañeras,* weddings, and baptisms.

Teresa and Julio arrived at the *quinceañera* to celebrate the introduction of new fifteen-year-old women into society, one of the most talked about social events of that spring. They sat at a table reserved by María Antonia for the rest of the family. Ana did not attend given her opinion about such celebrations.

The evening went remarkably smooth, and any reaction to seeing Julio, a dark-skinned Puerto Rican, dating a descendant of a well-to-do Spanish family was unnoticeable. However, Teresa anticipated the gossip that would spread about her future fiancé.

That evening at home, Teresa told Gabriela that if she had heard gossip, she wanted to know the content of the same, an attitude which surprised Gabriela.

"Then why did you go if you knew that might happen?"

"To prepare myself for when I marry Julio, because I want a big fancy wedding, nothing modest or simple. And I want to hold the reception there to show people what a mixed-race couple looks like in real life. I want to break color barriers in this community."

"You're still not worried about the mixed-race children you might have? People will call them *negritos.*"

"And that is a term of endearment most of the time, not a racial slur like in the States. I'm not worried at all."

"I admire you, and you will always have my support for your choices, Teresa."

* * *

Fernan Díaz got engaged to Noemí Pereira three years after having passed the Puerto Rico Bar Exam and having landed a job almost immediately with a small law firm named Rodríguez, Nolla, and Pérez.

He had been smitten by her large green eyes, flaxen black hair, and her caramel-colored skin tone. Her laughter was genuine and everyone seemed to like her, except his mother, Gabriela.

He didn't quite understand why. Noemí was educated, polite, and very outgoing. She made friends easily, so Fernan didn't comprehend the lack of chemistry between her and his mother. Perhaps it was because Noemí was raised in a home of privilege and spoke about it too often.

Nonetheless, his plans to marry Noemí were fixed, and they became engaged at his cousin's restaurant, the Casa Malatrasi, which had a private room for this type of function. All went well and Gabriela behaved, although she looked uneasy most of the time. Fernan had arranged the seats so she would sit as far as possible from Noemí, who was flanked by her parents. Gabriela had called her a *comemierda* and a very superficial being; nothing would change her mind, so he sat her near María Antonia.

A few months later, through a friend, he learned of an opening in the Puerto Rican Justice Department, the Civil Litigation unit, and it caught his attention. The only problem was that most likely the appointment would go to a political activist or their son or a person connected to the ruling party, which still was the New Palm Party. Perhaps that might change in the upcoming election, if he became more active with the Popular Democrats or switched allegiance and joined the Palms, something many others did, but he couldn't betray his personal ideals or politics just for a job.

The legal work at the small firm was satisfying to a point. He had hoped to practice financial law and represent a bank or a credit union, but the demand in his office was for family law, mostly divorces and alimony claims. Those matters soon became routine with no intellectual challenges. The law firm represented some small businesses, but only one community bank. The bank did not have enough litigation referrals to reach his desk.

A couple of luncheon appointments with a fellow attorney, who was already employed by the government, resulted in his renewed interest in the Justice Department.

At the third lunch with Miguel Sepúlveda, his law school classmate and friend came accompanied by a fellow coworker whom Fernan had never met. Her name was Linda Sepulveda, Miguel's cousin. She was a recent graduate from a private law school, part of the Caribbean American University.

At age 26, she had secured a job in the same office that Fernan had been thinking of applying to. She was strikingly beautiful, with reddish brown hair, light brown eyes, and carefully applied makeup which perfectly emphasized her features. Fernan felt an instant attraction to her delicate manner, and by how she pronounced certain words in English, since she mixed both languages frequently, much like some Nuyoricans he had met.

As she rose from the table to return to her office, she kissed Fernan on the cheek, in the Puerto Rican custom after meeting someone new but having established a connection.

Fernan hoped he could meet with her again, and later asked Miguel if she was married or engaged or seeing someone. Miguel replied that he didn't know for sure.

"She is quite a woman, Miguel," Fernan said as he took leave of his friend.

"I agree, and she is the loveliest woman in our family, believe me. But aren't you engaged?"

"Yes I am, but I'm not blind." He then asked for her phone number at work. Miguel gave him the general office number while staring quizzically at Fernan.

"Don't do anything that will come back to haunt you."

"Trust me. I won't."

A few weeks passed and Fernan summoned up the courage to call Linda and invite her to lunch in Old San Juan. She accepted and asked if Miguel was joining them, to which he replied no.

They met at Casa de España, a mansion built in the Andalusian architectural style, which was footsteps from the San Juan Bay. It had a restaurant on the second floor that had just reopened after a hiatus. It was almost empty.

She arrived on time and was dressed in high heels and a smart gray suit that reflected her figure in the right places. After the greeting, they sat down at a table near a window with an unobstructed view of the port. With that setting, it wouldn't be a quick lunch.

"Are you happy at your law firm, Fernan?" she started.

"Yes and no. My work is highly repetitive, and at times boring, but I'm treated well. And you?"

"I'm satisfied for now and challenged, but what I don't like is the attendance record of my fellow attorneys. They will leave for court early in the morning for the 9:00 a.m. calendar calls, and they never come back to the office. I've heard rumors that a few have private offices on the side, which is strictly prohibited."

"That doesn't surprise me. I've met some of those attorneys in local courts, appearing in cases which have nothing to do with the Justice Department. I heard that one attorney actually joined another law firm while on extended sick leave from a government agency."

"It's depressing and illegal, but I'm not shocked. To another subject. Where are you originally from?"

"I came to Puerto Rico as a child from Barcelona, but I've been a U.S. citizen since my 18th birthday. I chose to be one since this is my home now, and I gave up my right to be a Spanish citizen. My mother never did that."

"You still have a Catalonian accent."

"I know, and that won't go away. And you?"

"I was born in Cayey. My parents owned a bakery there, which was quite popular, and that business paid for my education all the way through law school."

"Are you taken?" he asked suddenly, then bit his tongue. *How foolish of me.*

Linda paused, not knowing where this line of questions would take them. She too, was attracted to Fernan, this boyish looking attorney much older than her, but very handsome and enticing.

"Are you?" she answered.

"I just got engaged a few weeks ago. Hope that doesn't affect our new friendship."

"It won't, if you continue to be honest. I like that, and I like you."

She touched his hand for emphasis. His pulse increased rapidly.

Part Three

Chapter 14
Consequences

P olitical turmoil increased at the beginning of the 1970s, with more daring and violent protests in picket lines against the insular and federal governments. The divided control of the local legislature didn't help, since it never set an example for real harmony and actual social progress.

The divisions in society were caused not only by the *independentistas* and other disaffected segments, but also by Red Popular fanatics set against Blue Palm followers. In jobs and family social gatherings, people were pitted against each other by party loyalties. Long-time friendships and family ties were strained, if not actually broken. After every election, the prevailing political party would clean house with faithful adherence to the "spoils system" which was ingrained in local government agencies—something the island, with all its problems, had not lived through before with such intensity.

In Puerto Rico, political discrimination became the original sin, much like racism in the States. A place, beloved by all and missed by millions of its migrants, now seemed like another planet. People returning from years living away didn't recognize the new order. A popular refrain was that you couldn't wait to get back to the beloved island, *mi bella isla,* until you couldn't wait to leave again.

Referendum after referendum on the island's status had resolved nothing, and it was clear to many, including some statehooders, that Congress was less than enthusiastic about admitting a new state with a primarily Spanish speaking population and a poverty-stricken economy.

Statehooders wouldn't stop fighting for that ideal, and kept on trying year after year, fruitlessly.

Within that dysfunctional scenario, Héctor evolved into a more radical proponent of the island's separation from the United States. In his group of sympathizers for island independence, there was an element that believed that once Congress responded to a petition for statehood by island voters, an improbable goal, and Congress rejected the results, the independence movement would be reborn and its followers would multiply.

"That is exactly what is going to happen," Héctor said to his group one evening at his apartment. "Let the statehooders win a plebiscite and petition Congress, then watch their reaction when Congress ignores or rejects the request."

"Well, Héctor, they will just try and try again like they say. Hawaii and Alaska did many times before they were admitted," Armando chimed in.

"But here it's different. In those cases, 80 or 85 percent of the population wanted statehood. The statehood movement in Puerto Rico barely has 45 percent of the votes for that status. It's not enough. The majority of the population doesn't want statehood."

The electorate, they hoped, would finally realize that Congress did not want the island as state of the union and would embrace independence. One of the governors elected, a member of the New Palm Party, actually said that if statehood was denied, he would become an independence sympathizer. No one believed him.

At the same time, some separatist groups tried even more daring acts of defiance, including attacks on federal property and sit-ins at the

University of Puerto Rico. One group in 1972, unaffiliated to Héctor and his associates, began a protest against the Army ROTC presence on campus, which resulted tragically in the death of an ROTC cadet.

Héctor rejected this strategy; he wanted no more deaths of innocents, even while some of his followers accepted those results as collateral damage. A strike against empty buildings for him was acceptable, but only where no one would get hurt. But that wasn't enough for some clandestine groups.

"See what I said? How are we going to win over people to our cause if we keep on killing innocents, especially students?" Héctor exclaimed when he read the news about the ROTC cadet, who was barely 20.

"Accidents happen, Héctor," Jesús Carrillo said. "I'm not afraid of any mistakes we may make." He had just joined the group of insurgents.

"I don't buy that."

Héctor suspected that some of those groups had been infiltrated by local authorities, mainly from intelligence units of the Commonwealth Police, or possibly the FBI. What he didn't realize was that his EPI group had also been infiltrated by an undercover police agent, who at times helped them plan subversive activities.

Armando López, a former Marine, was very skillful in hiding his true loyalties, so much that he tried at times to be the most aggressive member of EPI. He encouraged new approaches to counter government propaganda and joined every picket line he could.

After each event, he would report his activities to Lieutenant Néstor Espinosa, his commander at Hato Rey's main police headquarters.

Also, an affiliated group of independence believers was ready to attack the Air National Guard Base at the San Juan airport, specifically the fighter jets, plus some other target of the U.S military, but Héctor wasn't on board, so they all split into a separate faction and left the EPI.

* * *

Ana didn't expect the unannounced visit of Héctor one evening, He had called her to meet somewhere, but she felt safer at home, a place he preferred not to visit. But she told him it was her choice, not his.

"Sorry to show up with such short notice, *querida*, but I'm going away for a while," he said.

"Where to?" she asked.

"It's better that you not know. I think the authorities are watching my movements, and after that shooting at the UPR, I think it's just a matter of time before they arrest me for something I didn't do. That ROTC killing, I had nothing to do with it."

She noticed a tone of real regret in his words but said nothing about it. "And you expect me to believe you, or even care, with your history?"

"I guess not, but I wanted you to know I won't disappear from Carmencita's life, or yours, if you let me. I'll always be a part."

"A few years ago, I would have believed that you really cared about me. No longer. At least think about your baby daughter."

"I still have feelings for you, Ana, and I do love Carmencita."

"Yes, you have said that before, but you love your politics even more, even if it destroys our lives. If you continue like you have, she will lose a father. You forget that my brother was used and brainwashed by political forces, including my mother, at a tender young age. He paid for it with his life."

"Don't you believe in our cause? I thought you were a patriot."

"Of course I do and I am, but I'm not a criminal or an arsonist."

"That's not fair."

"Oh, yes it is. I think you should go, Héctor. We have nothing further to discuss." She began tearing up as she turned her back to him.

He walked away, but after a few steps looked back at the woman he had loved most in his life, one who was now lost to him.

Héctor walked slowly to the old Dos Hermanos bridge that connected the Condado to the isle of San Juan, and he stopped momentarily to view the ocean waves breaking against a rock that was shaped like a dog, which legend said was waiting for its master to return from the sea. The clear blue skies and the beach ringed by swaying palm trees provided a respite from his troubles.

His mind was full of conflicting thoughts. He wanted out, but only after one last symbolic, but memorable, strike against the state. Planning this operation would fill his days while he figured out an exit from his group of radicals, and then a possible reconciliation with Ana.

* * *

Fernan Díaz viewed the approaching wedding date for him and Noemí with trepidation. He had genuine feelings for her, but his friendship with Linda was getting complicated. She was all that Noemí was not. Alluring, distant, smart, complicated, and very opinionated as well. He liked all of that plus her natural sex appeal.

They had not gotten physical yet, in spite of their frequent meetings on Fridays after work—Social Fridays, as they were known on the island, where men and women would gather at local bars and hotel lounges to unwind and flirt.

They sometimes danced when there was live music, but that wasn't the purpose of their rendezvous. Fernan was 20 years older than Linda, but his youthful demeanor and build belied his age. Linda didn't ask his age, but she could guess.

Fernan met Linda one Friday night at a local hotel lobby bar. She said to him, "Fernan, what are we doing here? I am really fond of you, but you are taken, and I can still find someone else before it's too late."

"You are certainly beautiful, and I have no doubts about how easily you will find love. All you have to do is ask me to back off and I will."

"Are you still getting married around Christmas?"

"I'm not sure, but yes, that's the plan."

"And what happens to us? From that day forward you will not be part of my life, no matter how you and I feel about each other."

They had been slow dancing to a *bolero* and he reached down and kissed her full on the lips for the first time. She pulled away at first, but later responded in kind.

It was their first act of romantic love, much more than the flirtation they had had at the beginning, and it broke a dam of their pent-up feelings that had been harbored for more than six months.

They left the hotel lobby quickly and resumed their passionate kissing in his car, located in the underground parking of the Hotel San Jeronimo in the Condado.

"What now?" Linda asked when they stopped to catch their breaths.

"All I know is that I'm madly in love with you, yet face a difficult decision, since Noemí doesn't deserve this."

"Then tell her. Don't waste her time, or mine."

"It's not that easy. I will break her heart." Fernan let go of her and looked through the windshield at the empty cars in the garage. *What quicksand he had just stepped into.*

"Let's go. You have a lot of thinking to do, and don't call me until you've made up your mind," Linda said.

"Please listen to me. I think I love you. I didn't expect this would happen. You are being too harsh. Give me more time."

"Neither did I, but I can't be the other woman in your life. You need time, so here it is."

Linda stepped out of the car and walked towards her own vehicle parked a few yards away. She drove off without looking back. Fernan's heart sank as he saw her leave, but he couldn't imagine a scenario in which he would break his engagement with Noemí. *What would his mother think? What about other people? His friends would certainly be shocked, but that wasn't the most important thought.*

How would Noemí react? He started shivering, assuming it was the air conditioning in the garage.

* * *

Teresa and Julio planned a wedding for the summer of 1969. She would be 37 years old by then, not exactly the best marrying age, but she didn't care. That fact, plus the one that she was marrying a person of color, would make the social paper's headlines, which she antici- pated desperately.

She had held various jobs since graduating from college, but none had lasted more than two years. Julio had a new more challenging job as a tax preparation specialist in a private CPA firm. It was a bit boring and repetitive, but it gave him a safety net for emergencies. He was desperate to marry Teresa, a woman who had almost lost her life in the early 1950s.

At first, they thought about living together, something not socially accepted in the circles they moved in, and an action that would have produced a negative response from the entire family, mostly from Gabriela, now in her golden years.

They rented an apartment, but told no one, and began furnishing it well before their nuptials. Julio paid the rent since the lease was in his name, but for the time being lived with his parents, as did Teresa. Some weekends they would meet in the apartment located in Rio Piedras and decorate, plus much more.

The wedding day came, and the ceremony was held in La Merced church on Hato Rey. As planned, they held the bridal reception in the Condado Casino. Invitations were sent out to 100 guests, including almost all of their friends and acquaintances as well as members of María Antonia's inner circle in the New Palm Party. Only 40 persons showed up, a fear that Gabriela and Teresa had harbored. RSVPs were received from many families claiming a conflict for one reason or another.

Teresa didn't let that fact ruin her celebration, but she told her mother that she no longer wanted anything to do with those phony friends.

Julio's parents were present, as was his immediate family, although they felt out of place in such surroundings. All the descendants of the Roche family were there as well.

Edwin Ferrer attended the reception at the invitation of Carlos and María Antonia, who were contributing funds for the wedding costs to help Gabriela. He found the wedding lavish, something he could never afford even if he remarried someday. No one there knew him except the wedding couple and Carlos and María Antonia. He sat at a table with people who were friendly and welcoming.

Fernan realized at the wedding that his turn would come soon, but complications in life can arise unexpectedly. His wedding, he surmised, would be even fancier than Teresa's. At least he hoped it would, if he got a better job than his current one. He had applied to become a District Attorney in the Justice Department, after giving up on chances to join the Civil Litigation unit. It would be only trying criminal cases, however, which he once hoped to avoid.

Ana Roche was present as well, with her little daughter Carmencita, who was now almost 5 years old. At the reception, María Antonia introduced her to Francisco Rovira, a fellow teacher at the university. She thought he might make a good match for Ana, even though she had a little girl and was now a working mother.

Francisco and Ana talked for a lengthy period of time at the reception; she didn't dance, neither did he. He was able to relate to Carmencita easily, a good sign.

* * *

Edwin had been successful in turning around the fortunes of the Malatrasi eatery. He began with the name change to Casa Malatrasi, evoking a future inn that would be emerging from an old relic of a building on Calle Cruz. The inn wouldn't compete with any major hotel in the city, but would rather be a cozy, intimate boutique hotel catering to discerning tourists. It would not have a casino or gambling of any type, and no disco or music venue, just a small, elegant bar in the recesses of the lobby and another smaller bar on the rooftop adjacent to a swimming pool.

Carlos Roche had bought out the interest of Manuel Malatrasi, who retired, and then discarded the idea of naming the new inn Hotel Central, a name suggested by the former owner. It was too plain and cold.

Edwin made the decision to manage both businesses, which left him little free time for diversions or entertainment. He had promoted Ruben to be the assistant manager, but gave him no record keeping responsibilities.

He continued dating Laura but had not broached the subject of marriage or an engagement. To him, courting a widow was unfamiliar, but being a widower helped him understand that time cured all wounds, as they said. He didn't doubt how much he loved this new version of Laura.

* * *

Ruben Collado had almost forgotten about his unresolved debts to the drug dealers of New York, since he had not heard from them in 18 months, and when previously contacted, he had ignored their messages. He assumed they had forgotten about him. Early one morning, a messenger appeared at the door of the restaurant and handed him a note.

It read:

> We know where you work, we know where you live. Meet us at 10 p.m. tomorrow night at the plaza behind San Jose Church. Come alone and bring the money you owe (not the product) or else. — Your Nuyorican compadres

A flash of fear passed through Ruben. Should he heed the warning? How could they possibly know where he worked or lived?

He didn't have the product anymore. Half of it was unsellable, he had discovered, when he opened the package and saw a ball of white powder which definitely was not marijuana. More like heroin, or something else. He had been able to sell some of it anyway, but the rest he disposed of in a trash can on the sidewalk near his bus stop in Rio Piedras. He saved the small amount of cash he obtained as insurance for a rainy day.

Now they were here, and his stash was less than $5,000, but he hoped that would be enough for his adversaries.

Not wanting to complicate matters further, he took the cash out of the hiding place he had created in the restaurant kitchen and put the white paper envelope in a brown shopping bag.

That night at the designated hour, he arrived at the front of the church and looked for anyone standing nearby. The plaza was deserted, the only noises coming from a group of patrons at a restaurant bar across the street.

Soon a dark red car showed up with three occupants. One of them got out and walked over to Ruben. He signaled to have Ruben follow him to the rear of the church.

"Do you have the money?" the man asked.

"Yes, it's almost all there, Ruben said.

The stranger took the bag and looked at the envelope. He began flipping through the cash, then stopped and asked, "How much is this?"

"Around 5,000 dollars."

"That's less than half of what you owe. Where is the rest?"

"The white powder you gave me was ruined by the time I arrived here from New York. It was no good."

"And you expect us to believe that, *cabrón?*"

"It's the truth."

"You have until next week to get the rest, or you will pay dearly, *hijo de puta.*" The man showed Ruben a weapon he had in his pocket, then spun around and headed back to the waiting vehicle.

Ruben realized that this was not an empty threat. It could cost him his life. He shook inside, stepped into the shadows of the church, and returned to Casa Malatrasi following a different route.

Chapter 15
Cerro El Torito

O n the mountain road of old Route 15, four miles up from Cayey towards the town of Guayama where the main road veers off, there was an unpaved mountain trail. This path led to five acres of undeveloped land which ended in a rocky promontory overlooking the southeast coast of the island. On those unspoiled emerald acres, there were two giant steel towers, one for the electric power lines that supply energy to the southeast coast of Puerto Rico, and another tower functioning as a radio and television retransmission antenna for the public TV station in San Juan.

That is where Héctor Estrada and his group planned their next disruption of normal life for the island. They were not out to seek a brief temporary disruption, but a more lasting one that would spread their revolutionary message throughout Puerto Rico. The towers were not guarded constantly; just one watchman inspected the towers twice a day, early in the morning and right after dusk.

Héctor made various scouting trips to *El Torito*, as the point was affectionately nicknamed for the bullhead shaped stone rock, with the excuse that he would spend time in a *bohío* type café bar specializing in *criollo* food. The towers were less than a mile away; one could almost walk to them.

The plans were to be kept highly secret, with only Héctor, Armando López, and the new recruit Jesús Carillo informed of the details. It was supposed to be foolproof. No one else would learn of the date and time of the planned sabotage. The three men would approach the site after 10:00 p.m., first ascertaining that no sentry was present.

Once that was done, they would then unload the explosives. They had acquired various sticks of dynamite from criminal sources and would carry them in knapsacks on a footpath for the last 150 yards. This path led directly to the towers.

Jesús was charged with cutting open the wire fence to gain access to the enclosure. After they unloaded the dynamite, they would attach an extra-long cable to the explosives and put a timer on the igniter switch at the end.

If all went according to plan, they would have plenty of time to scamper down the earthen road, climb aboard their Jeep, and leave the area safely. That was the plan; it seemed that Héctor's idea of no lives lost and no one hurt would transpire without incident.

The night before the planned sabotage, the crew met to discuss final details. The car that they planned to use had to belong to someone unconnected to them, so a theft was planned of an older model Jeep that they had spotted in a commercial parking lot adjoining a supermarket. It was there all day every day, except on Fridays, and apparently it belonged to an employee of the market.

The date chosen for the attack was on July 4th, 1970, a Saturday, and the start of long holiday weekend. Every minute detail was reviewed, including what to wear, like masks, hats, gloves, and the proper shoes. Weapons were discussed, but only two of the men, Héctor and Armando, had revolvers, and that was deemed sufficient. Emergency exit plans were discussed, but not in too much detail since the towers had only one way out. Forests and brushes blocked all other exit possibilities.

The stage was set for the event. Héctor announced that this was his last operation. He was a father now, and jobless. The other two members of the team didn't react to his revelation.

* * *

Armando López had already told Lieutenant Espinosa of the operation being planned. The officer had organized a welcome committee for that night with eight police officers, including a sergeant and himself, all armed with service revolvers and light automatic weapons.

"Are you certain that this bombing will happen on July 4th at exactly ten?" Lieutenant Espinosa asked.

"*Claro*, I am sure," Armando said.

"Only the three of you? Seems like a small team for such a task."

"Just us three. Will I be safe given the circumstances?"

"I've informed the others that you are undercover."

"But what if a gunfight starts and bullets fly? What should I do?"

"No worries. There won't be shots fired. If there were, I personally will look out for you. It's just a warning, to scare them for good. It's not a plan to kill terrorists, even though they deserve that and much more."

"As long as no one dies or is badly wounded, then that's okay."

"Just as long as they don't fire at us, it won't happen," Espinosa said, slapping Armando on the back for reassurance.

"Remember, Lieutenant," Armando said, "these are not soldiers. They are amateurs who believe in a cause, erroneous as it may be."

"Still, they like playing with fire, and this is a terrorist act, no matter how you view it."

* * *

Edwin had noticed a change Ruben's demeanor. He often arrived late, was frequently distracted, and had a hard time remembering instructions, including specials of the day, and certain dinner reservations.

Casa Malatrasi had come into better times with the reorganization of the kitchen and waitstaff. Edwin had also had the dining room redecorated. He had eliminated the taped background monotonous bullfight music and brought in small bands on weekends to play modern songs, mostly Spanish romantic ballads. These changes brought a younger crowd to dine, who also liked to spend more and stay longer.

So Ruben's attitude puzzled Edwin and he sat down with him one morning after he arrived an hour late.

"Ruben, there is something troubling you? How can I help?"

"*No es nada*, don't worry, I can manage."

"Well, I do worry, because in less than a year I promoted you to head waiter and maître'd, and you're screwing up."

"I have some minor problems to fix, but I have them under control."

"It doesn't seem like it, Ruben. We are family. You can tell me anything, no matter what, believe me."

"It won't interfere with my job, I assure you, Edwin."

All Ruben could think about was how to avoid another encounter with the New York gang, most of whom had returned to New York but no doubt had left accomplices in San Juan in charge of collecting his debt.

"It had better not," Edwin responded curtly. "Don't make me choose between you and the restaurant, please." He stood up and went back to his office.

Ruben contemplated his choices. For a brief moment he even had thought of "borrowing" funds from the restaurant's cash vault for a short time and later slowly repaying the funds. That choice would be a betrayal of Edwin's trust, and Ruben had no idea how long the missing cash would remain unnoticed, or how long it would take him to replace it. He dismissed the thought outright; he could never do that and would take his chances.

* * *

On Sunday, July 3rd, Héctor made another unplanned, unannounced visit to Ana at home. She was tending the garden, and playing with Carmencita, who let go with a yelp of glee when she saw him.

"What a surprise," Ana said when she turned around to see why her daughter had laughed.

"I thought I'd come by, if it's okay."

"I suppose so, but I would have like some prior notice."

"I may have to travel out of Puerto Rico for some time," he said as he tussled Carmencita's hair.

"You said that before. *Que pasa?*"

"I need to work at something that will pay me enough for you and Carmencita."

"As for me, don't worry. But yes, your daughter is another matter."

"That's why I have to leave."

"There is work here in San Juan, isn't there?"

"Not the type I'm looking for. A Social Sciences major is not in high demand in the job market."

"When will you leave?"

"Soon. As early as next week."

"So this is goodbye then?"

"I imagine so, at least for a while."

"Can you tell me where you might go?"

"Maybe Miami or Boston."

"Two very different cities, and very different people and climates."

"I'm aware. But I know many persons who have benefitted from leaving the island."

Héctor spent a few hours with Carmencita while Ana tended her garden chores, then later approached both of them and said his good-byes. He hugged his daughter tightly, so tight that she wriggled to get loose. He put her down after kissing her, then stepped over to Ana and gave her a kiss on the cheek.

* * *

Monday, July 4th was a day that had produced perfect weather on the island. Temperatures hovered near 90 degrees, and there was a cloud-less sky.

Héctor decided that morning, on his own, to drive by the group's intended target. The drive was uneventful, but on his way up the mountain range, as he passed the sideroad to the towers, he noticed a small white VW Beetle sedan parked at the entrance. This caused him some concern; there wasn't supposed to be anyone at the site at that hour.

He stopped his car 100 yards further up the highway and waited to see who the occupants of the VW might be. As he waited, he reviewed the details of the attack, not forgetting about the escape plan after the bombing. He had decided they should wait at a safe distance after the explosions to make sure the towers were destroyed, avoiding the failure of the Monacillos Molotov cocktail bombing.

After half an hour, Héctor saw two men approach the VW and get in. They put the car in reverse, backed out of the dirt road entrance, and drove down the mountain. Héctor observed them through his rearview mirror and assumed that the men hadn't seen him.

Were they extra watchmen, employees of the Fuentes Fluviales, the power company, or from another company? They couldn't be police, since they didn't have uniforms, nor were they dressed like detectives.

His group would move forward with the plans, notwithstanding this unexpected development.

Héctor failed to inform his men what he had witnessed earlier that day as he reviewed the operation in detail. Armando López kept asking questions about the exact time of the attack, as if he were preparing for a dress rehearsal.

Nightfall came with a spectacular Caribbean Sea sunset.

Armando had extensive military training, since he had served two years in the Marine Corps, leaving the service only after his father died and leaving his family destitute in Fajardo, Puerto Rico. He took a hardship discharge and returned to the island, where he joined the police force. After a year, he was assigned to the Special Investigations Unit at headquarters. A burly man, weighing 180 pounds of mostly muscle, he had a commanding presence notwithstanding that he was only 5 foot 5 inches tall. He walked vigorously even over short distances, as if he were marching in formation.

Raised in nearly abject poverty, he was a staunch believer that the Americans had saved Puerto Rico from itself, in providing many social and economic benefits missing in other Caribbean islands and in many Central American countries. Any association or entity that preached independence, by force or by vote, was to him anti-American and had to be dealt with, with no limitations.

He was not particularly violent, but rather thought that enemies of the U.S. could be defeated in other ways. This provided his motivation to infiltrate separatist groups and thwart their plans of sabotage or violence. For him, loyalty and honor were the most important virtues learned in the Marines. Funny thing was that he had stayed away from politics of any kind.

When he realized that the plans for El Torito were imminent and would indeed be carried out, he communicated with his superiors in Hato Rey, using a walkie talkie hidden in his home.

He still had second thoughts about how it would go down. In spite of his beliefs, he had grown fond of this ragtag group of separatists, who were not criminals in the ordinary sense, but were ready to commit and justify illicit acts for the sake of *patria*. They were idealists without a justifiable cause.

Armando liked how Héctor would carefully listen to everyone's opinion before an event, since their activities posed unintended consequences and calculated risks of bodily harm to everyone, including himself. But mostly it was always Héctor's decision that carried the day.

On the night of July 4th, Armando made one last call to his superior to make sure that all their plans were ready. The police, he was told, would be hidden behind the guard house of the towers and in the surrounding bushes. The squad had been reduced to only six cops for security reasons. These were the most trusted members of Lt. Espinosa's squad in the Intelligence Division. Armando was reassured once again, at his request, that this was only a warning. His team would not be hurt if they surrendered peacefully.

* * *

Héctor and his crew met at his house at 7:30 p.m. and together drove to the Cayey-Guayama destination along Highway 1. They avoided the new expressway that was being constructed from the exit of Río Piedras to the town of Caguas.

Having reached their target, they waited patiently for the appointed hour inside the Jeep they had stolen from El Comandante Shopping Center. The license plates had been swapped in an attempt to fool the authorities.

At the exact hour at Cerro El Torito, Héctor and his men left the Jeep and walked 60 yards to the entrance of the two giant towers. They surveyed the scene and, believing it safe, proceeded with their mission.

Jesús Carillo cut a large hole in the wire fence, big enough for each of them to crawl through. Armando, due his girth, had the most difficulty fitting through the hole. Once in, they walked to the designated areas to place the dynamite in two separate locations.

Suddenly ten paces away from their targets, several bright spotlights illuminated them and they heard the words, "*Alto*, stop right there, or we will shoot."

Héctor reached for his pistol, a .38 caliber revolver and pointed it at the talking shadows but didn't shoot. Then he heard a command, "We have you surrounded, *cabrones,* so don't even think about it."

Armando hadn't drawn his 9mm pistol, and hesitated. Suddenly a shot ran out, an errant one that hit Héctor in his right upper shoulder. Héctor attempted to fire his revolver, but the gun jammed. Then six policeman jumped out of their hiding places after firing above the heads of the interlopers and surrounded the three men.

"Get on your knees, *pendejos*," shouted Sergeant Miguel Acosta, a 10-year veteran of the Commonwealth Police Force.

Héctor, Armando, and Jesús obeyed, and the latter started pleading for his life.

"*Por favor no me maten.* Don't shoot!" Jesús cried out as his tears began flowing.

"So you *maricones* thought that you could advance your struggle by destroying government property and causing a massive blackout of electric power and TV?"

Héctor remained silent, but Armando, in a mock plea, said, "We have learned our lesson, so let's go back to Cayey and face a judge. I will call my attorney."

Armando's words sounded rehearsed, and it raised Héctor's suspicions. *How had they known the exact time and location of their mission?* He then remembered the two men he had seen there earlier in the day and Armando's insistence on the exact time of the attack. *They must have been advance undercover agents.*

"*Mierda*, you will call no one," the sergeant said. All this time, Lt. Espinosa was looking at Armando with a sadistic smile.

Héctor said nothing. His shoulder was bleeding profusely now. This wasn't just a scratch.

"You so-called *patriotas* are what's wrong with this country, lessons learned my ass," Espinosa stated angrily.

He walked over to Armando, and with the butt of his automatic weapon hit his undercover agent in the head, knocking him out. This had not been rehearsed.

"Get him out of here," he instructed two of his men, pointing to Armando.

"What is going to happen to us?" Héctor asked.

Jesús Carrillo was whimpering on his knees, but he hadn't been hurt yet. It was at that moment that Héctor realized that Armando was an undercover agent. *How stupid could I have been to trust him?*

"What are we gonna do with them?" Sergeant Acosta said as he placed handcuffs on the two men. He had handed Héctor a small cloth to stem the blood before cuffing him.

"We deal with them here. I have orders from higher ups that they not leave here in one piece," Espinosa answered.

"You mustn't mean what I'm thinking. They have surrendered and are now unarmed. Have you thought this out?" Sergeant Acosta exclaimed.

"I have my orders, and if anyone here disagrees with me, you can leave right now," Espinosa shouted. No one moved.

Sergeant Acosta couldn't believe his ears. He hated saboteurs, but he hadn't planned on killing them. That would be the end of his career, and maybe even prison. For his own benefit, he took photos with a small camera while the men were on their knees.

Espinosa saw him, but did nothing.

Héctor understood what would happen next. He was wounded and would not be leaving alive. Jesús was now crying loudly and cursing the cops, thinking how foolish he had been in not fearing any consequences.

Moments passed and one policeman, Corporal Sergio Andrade, approached the two men, looked at Lt. Espinosa for confirmation, pulled out his service revolver and shot both Héctor and Jesús point blank in the face. He tried to replicate a frontal bullet wound, as would happen in an exchange of gunfire.

He went over to Héctor's prone body, picked up his revolver, removed and reloaded the bullets, and then fired into the air, later picking up the shell casings.

A few policemen looked away, understanding the repercussions of what had just happened. They had committed murder.

Sgt. Acosta took photos of the dead men. Corporal Andrade asked if it wouldn't be better to just dispose of the bodies in a hidden grave.

Acosta couldn't believe his ears. "Are you crazy? How can we explain a shootout without corpses? And trust me, we will have a lot of explaining to do."

The bodies of Héctor and Jesús were stuck in the trunks of two separate police cruisers and taken away to the nearest town morgue. Explanations would be necessary; newspapers would write stories and the bodies would be photographed. Sgt. Acosta was right, and he now possessed crucial damning evidence of the deed.

* * *

When Armando awakened later at a local dispensary, with a nasty bump on his head, he asked the others what had transpired.

Lt. Espinosa fudged his answer and said that the two terrorists had pulled out another weapon from their trouser legs and had been killed in the exchange of gunfire which ensued.

Armando didn't believe him. He realized that now he was an accessory to a planned assassination.

Chapter 16

Repercussions

Ana awoke the morning of July 7th to the TV news that a terrorist act had been stopped the night before in the central mountain range of the island, near Cayey. Exact details were not provided, since this was a morning broadcast and more news was expected later. The police superintendent would give a television briefing later that morning, according to the Telemundo reporter.

Immediately, Ana hoped that the incident, which had been thwarted by the police, did not involve Héctor or anyone associated with him, but she knew this was a false hope.

She hurriedly did her chores and tended to Carmencita, and when finished she went to the main house to speak to Carlos Roche, now in his late eighties and retired from all political activity. She was prepared on how to break the news in the event he hadn't heard.

By the time she saw Carlos, he had seen the first broadcast and asked her if the purported act had anything to do with Héctor, the father of her child. She replied that she didn't think so, since he was leaving the island headed to the U.S. on a job search, according to what he had last told her.

"Good," Carlos said, changing the tone of his voice to a more relaxed one. "It would be terrible if he was involved. Have you spoken to him lately?"

"No," she answered, avoiding his eyes.

"Then let's wait to see what really happened. I don't trust the police version of anything connected to terrorism. Did you know that after more than a decade and a half they found the bullet that wounded your cousin, Teresa, in 1950?"

"No, I didn't know," Ana gasped.

"Because they told no one that it was a bullet fired from a standard police revolver. I found out thanks to a contact in the police lab. The final report was destroyed soon after the discovery."

"Does Teresa know this?"

"No, and it makes no sense to tell her now and have her relive that day."

"I agree," Ana replied.

There were no police briefings that morning. They had been cancelled, according to the bulletins on TV.

The new daily newspaper, the San Juan *Gazette*, was the first to get photos from an unidentified source and ran a story. Two weeks after the killings, someone had leaked photos of the two men lying dead on the turf of El Torito, with bullet holes in their faces. The photos showed an ugly bloody horrific scene depicting of the events of the night of July 4th. The victims' faces were mangled and not easily distinguishable.

The front-page headline read:

POLICE STOP SUBVERSIVE PLOT AND KILL PERPETRATORS
UNANSWERED QUESTIONS PERSIST

The Police Commander of the Intelligence Unit in San Juan saw the headline and was furious.

He called Lt. Espinosa into his office to demand an explanation of that night's events, now displayed on the front page of all the island's major newspapers with the photos.

"What the hell is this?" Colonel Juan García shouted at Lt. Espinosa. "That wasn't what we discussed when planning the capture of the terrorists. It now appears like an ambush. How do we explain that?"

"The pictures were taken by Sergeant Acosta, who swears he didn't leak them."

"Then who did, and who authorized taking the photos? Do you realize how that makes us look? Why didn't you confiscate the camera at the time, *idiota?*"

"I thought the pictures might be useful in an investigation on what actually went down."

"Are you stupid, or do you just act like a moron? Of course they will be useful—for all the subversives out there, their sympathizers, and the island's socialist press."

Lt. Espinosa was at a loss for words, but said, "I was told by you and Lt. Colonel Marrero not to let them leave the area of the intended bombing under any circumstances."

"Did you understand that to mean kill them right there?"

Espinosa didn't answer.

"I too, report to higher authority, you know. Prepare yourself for the storm and the flood of court hearings that will hit us, especially you. Put Sergeant Acosta on leave until the identity of the leaker is revealed."

"That's going to look like punishment without facts pointing to him."

"I don't care," García replied.

* * *

Ana couldn't believe it when she saw Héctor's destroyed face in the press. She started crying uncontrollably, so loud that María Antonia came running to see what was wrong.

She showed María Antonia the front page and María sat down, stifling her reaction. She had met Héctor a few times and almost liked him, regardless of his politics. What had happened was unforgivable.

"Try and calm down, Ana. It wasn't your fault, nor could you have prevented it."

* * *

Edwin read the latest news about Cerro El Torito and wasn't surprised by the attempted attack on the towers; what surprised him was the outcome. He had met Héctor Estrada, who seemed agreeable and nice, but if he was involved, especially as the father of Carlos's granddaughter, it would be terrible matter for that family to deal with. But he had other matters to worry about.

While the restaurant was profitable, it wasn't doing well enough to continue investing on the remodeling of the building that would later be known as the Casa Malatrasi hotel.

The initial investment was enormous, but doable; he hoped that if the recent successes of the restaurant continued, it would tide them over to finish the project.

But an issue that worried him more was that it seemed like the service at the eatery was beginning to falter. It was due to the inattentiveness of his manager, Ruben Collado. Casa Malatrasi received its first bad review from a well-known food critic, when previously it had received rave reviews from him and other food critics in San Juan. The bad review focused on the service, not on the food. Edwin had spoken to Ruben about the matter, but nothing had changed.

* * *

Ruben ignored the warnings of those in San Juan left in charge of collecting his drug debt. These local guys weren't teenagers like those he dealt with in New York. They were grown men and well known in the community as bullies. Most of them were known for their criminal records.

The three men actually entered the restaurant one night on a busy Friday, sat down at a table, and ran up a huge tab on food and drinks. Ruben greeted them nervously but knew they wouldn't create a scene with so many witnesses. After consuming all the food and expensive liquor to their satisfaction, they asked for the check, and when it arrived, wrote on the back:

IOU from your associates, will pay as you soon as you pay us. See you pronto. — Your buddies

All three men walked out smiling.

At the end of the night, when the accounts were tabulated, Ruben paid for the check from his own pocket, hoping to never see them again. It was wishful thinking.

A month later, Ruben was walking back to his apartment from the bus station when a car stopped in front of him on the deserted street and the same men stepped out of it and approached.

They called out to Ruben, "*Mira chico,* come here."

The tallest of them all, a man named Mickey, with tattoos on both his arms and neck, spoke to him from several feet away. "You have had more than enough time to pay the money you owe, and *mis amigos* in the big city are very impatient. So this your last warning. I was told to take any action needed. By the way the food where you work was delicious, thank you."

As Mickey turned away from him, Ruben blurted out, "I told you before, I no longer have the product, and I gave you all the money I had. Go to hell, assholes. Don't come back to the restaurant or I'll call the cops."

They all laughed at his remark, except Mickey. As Ruben turned his back on them, after giving them the middle finger, Mickey pulled out a gun and shot Ruben in the back.

* * *

Fernan had landed the job he applied for in the Justice Department, but as a district attorney, not in the civil litigation division he had hoped for. Now with a foot in the door, he figured a transfer to civil matters would be easier to get.

Once the news got out that there had been an attempted terrorist act in the central mountain range, he immediately wondered if Ana's boyfriend was involved.

There would be an investigation of the facts and how the young men had died. That was inevitable, but it shouldn't affect his duties.

He was wrong. As the shooting erupted into a full-fledged scandal, a special unit in the Criminal Division was created, to which many Assistant DAs from several offices were assigned. He was one of them.

At first, he was going to point out to his new bosses his relationship to one of the men, if it turned out to be Héctor. Then later, when he found out it was him, he decided to not reveal what he knew. One could not predict the speculation that it might create. Plus this was a career-defining moment and opportunity, and he didn't want to be sidelined.

The newspaper headlines finally identified the deceased men by name, age, and residence a month after the shooting. Héctor's picture was on the front page of three major newspapers. Two large photos appeared side by side, one from his driver's license, in black and white, the other in color, with his face mutilated by a bullet wound. It was ghastly.

Later a different newspaper headline appeared in San Juan's *El Imparcial*:

RADICAL SEPARATISTS KILLED, SOME DESCRIBE AS AMBUSH

Other news outlets ran the same headline with minor modifications.

Fernan instantly thought about Ana, but he refrained from calling her from his office. He would wait until he could talk to her in person. She would be distraught, so he waited a few days before visiting her in El Condado.

He was now living in Hato Rey in a condo apartment located in a newly built Condominium Tower just off Las Americas Expressway. He had married Noemí, reluctantly, while still having feelings for Linda Sepulveda, but he believed that she was now in his past. A forgotten love affair which never came about. Yet he couldn't stop thinking about her, even as a newlywed on his honeymoon.

Noemí was the ideal model for a beauty advertisement, slender and delicate with all the right moves. Her world was fashion, and she wasn't shy about buying the latest clothes the market brought to San Juan. Shopping centers were her main focus, and at one point she thought of leaving her office job to dedicate her talents to designing clothes for young women. She had an impenetrable shield about her, letting in only those whom she trusted. Fernan felt, many times, that he was on the outside looking in.

He hadn't seen Ana in more than a month, so when he met her at her home, he was astonished at her appearance. Large dark bags under her eyes, unkempt hair, and no makeup.

"*Ana, como estás?*"

"*Bien,* I suppose," she said.

"I saw the news, and I know that even with your breakup, it must be very hard."

"More than you can imagine. I warned him about possible consequences of his activities; violence, jail time, and the rest."

"I'm sorry, really sorry for you and Carmencita."

"She has no father now to help raise her."

"Whatever you need from us, just ask."

"Will you be involved in the investigation on what happened? I can't imagine Héctor shooting a police officer."

"Right now I don't know, it's possible. But I wouldn't be able to give you any inside information, anyway."

"I guess not," she said.

"Just keep reading the news and watching TV reports. This won't go away quietly. All I can say right now is that there are those who believe that this was a planned execution, not a real gunfight, not even an accident."

"I would not be surprised, after what Carlos Roche told me about your sister's shooting in 1950."

"What was that?"

"Ask him for the details."

* * *

The death of the separatists erupted into a widespread scandal with political opponents from both sides decrying it. At the beginning, many conservatives thought it was made up; then they said if it was real, the subversives deserved it. The more sensible populace called for an investigation that would reveal the truth, and who might be responsible for ordering the killing of the two *independentistas*.

The local Justice Department called for an in-depth investigation, which was hurriedly concluded in less than six weeks, and it found that the members of the Commonwealth Police were not at fault and had fired in self-defense. The FBI was added as an investigatory agency, and they also quickly cleared the police from any wrongdoing.

* * *

Armando López read the news and watched the TV coverage silently, but he couldn't sleep at night, thinking about his role in the El Torito massacre. He confided in no one, least of all his superiors in the Investigative Unit of the Police Department. He spoke as little as possible when asked by his family if he had been part of the operation that fateful July 4th. When he heard about how the police were absolved by the different investigative agencies, he knew he must act, even if it was career ending. They were covering up the truth, and he doubted that anyone would believe what he knew, even if they were told.

He kept a newspaper clipping of a headline in his desk at home and read it daily, as if the words would change when reviewed repeatedly.

The authorities might offer a deal for his testimony. Anything they offered would be okay; a short jail sentence which he deemed inevitable he could handle, since he felt he was a participant in the trap the police planned. His parents were not the type he could seek advice from, and neither was he a religious person who could turn to a priest.

He needed a friend, a good friend whom he could trust, one who wouldn't betray him. An uncle on his mother's side who was a veteran police officer seemed the best choice to confide in. The uncle had retired with the rank of Sergeant Major after working his way up the ranks with only a high school diploma. Armando pondered his next step.

*   *   *

The elections of 1972 produced a change in the island's government. The new Senate, with a Popular Democratic Party majority, set in place plans for Senate investigative hearings, to be televised, and named an independent prosecutor to handle them. Up until then no one had been officially accused of any misdeeds for the El Torito affair.

A witnesses' list was created by the Senate Committee, and subpoenas were sent out to each witness. The refusal of some policemen to testify was litigated in the local San Juan Superior Court by the appointed Senate prosecutor. Some of the key witnesses, three of the patrolmen present at the killing, fought the subpoenas all the way to the Commonwealth Supreme Court, while others capitulated and agreed to testify. Attorney's fees were mounting by the day, and the Policeman's Union would not cover all of the legal fees in the defense of the witnesses, so deals were made in exchange for testimony.

A subpoena was served on Armando López in his office in the main police headquarters in Hato Rey. Since the incident, he had been assigned duties at the Intelligence desk. The time had come for him to make a decision.

He went to visit his uncle, Esteban Urrutia, a native of Humacao and a longtime favorite of his. Armando worshipped Don Esteban and his sound advice whenever he needed to ask for help.

He hadn't seen his uncle for about six months and had never divulged the facts of his undercover work with the police. This wasn't the time for secrets, he thought. He must tell his uncle everything, warts and all.

Don Esteban was a grizzled veteran of the Humacao Police force and sported long gray sideburns that contrasted with his sunburnt face and balding scalp. He was now a dedicated fisherman spending most of his waking hours at sea in a small 16-foot schooner.

Armando arrived at his uncle's beachfront house early one Sunday morning, a few days after he was served with the Senate subpoena.

Two of his acquaintances in the Intelligence Division had offered to help and find an attorney that would represent him, partly paid for by the Police Union. He declined to accept their offer especially when he heard them say, "We are counting on you, as the only person alive of the three suspects who were there that night. We must stick together and get this right." For him, that was a veiled threat that he must toe the party line and not tell the truth.

"*Tio*, it's good to see you, even though this is not really a social visit."

His uncle hugged him, then welcomed him and asked that he sit down. "It doesn't matter, social or not. You are here."

"I'm in trouble, *Tio*. I was and still am an undercover cop for the Intelligence Division and I took part in an operation that went bad. Do you know about Cerro El Torito?"

"Who doesn't, on the entire island?"

"I was there."

"What?"

"I'll tell you the whole story."

After recounting the entire operation from start to finish, Armando paused to let the narrative sink in., then said, "And now, *Tio*, I have been summoned as a witness to those horrific events. The police probably want me to lie on the stand. It's the first time anyone has asked for my version. My identity has remained secret for all this time under the pretext, headquarters said, that as an undercover cop I would be put in mortal danger if my identity was revealed."

Esteban looked puzzled. "That's probably true. So what are you going to do?"

"That's the reason I'm here. I can't perjure myself. That's not what I was taught in the Marines or at the police academy. But my career as a cop is over, if I tell the truth. I love what I do, but no job is worth lying about the killing of two men. I wasn't even conscious when the actual shooting happened. I had been knocked out by a blow from a rifle butt to conceal my identity as an undercover."

"Armando, my beloved nephew, your career as a cop has come to an end anyway, tell the truth or not. It's your call on how you want to live the rest of your life. If you lie to protect your fellow officers, how will you feel afterwards, if they are acquitted from any charges? How long will their gratitude last? And even if they are found guilty, what comes next for you? What about the next time something like this happens? And mark my words, it will."

"I've thought about all of that, *Tio*."

"Then do what your conscience tells you. Do the right thing."

At this juncture, Armando, the tough Marine who had teared up during the exchange, started weeping quietly.

* * *

In July 1973, three years after the original plan to bomb El Torito, the Senate hearings began at the Capitol Building in San Juan, which faces the Atlantic Ocean and has unparalleled views of the sea. Waves crash in all their majesty at the very foot of the cliff across from the Capitol steps on Ponce De Leon Avenue. It was ironic that in such a beautiful setting, with a magnificent blend of sand, sea, and azure sky, a real-life murder mystery was now playing out on island-wide television.

Armando decided to comply with the Senate subpoena and testify. He had consulted a lawyer, and she was with him on the first day of his testimony. He needed her advice on how to deliver his testimony once he knew what to say.

He was the last witness to be called that was present at the killing of Héctor Estrada and Jesús Carillo. He made it clear in his testimony that he was knocked out when the actual shooting started, but he could testify as to what he witnessed prior to being knocked out.

The hearing room was packed. It hadn't been widely publicized who Armando actually was, just that he was an eyewitness. The previous witness that morning was a forensic examiner, an expert brought down from Washington D.C., who had testified, with visual charts, that the shots were fired from an angle, which the trajectory confirmed, and the men killed were on their knees.

Armando took the stand, was sworn in, and testified for six hours, with only two 20-minute bathroom breaks.

The prosecutor, Jacinto Ayala, an experienced former district attorney now in private practice but appointed by the Senate to lead the investigation, questioned Armando.

Once Armando stated that he was an undercover cop assigned to infiltrate groups which advocated violence in achieving independence for Puerto Rico, a gasp was heard throughout the audience.

"We have listened to your testimony, Mister López, up until the moment you were knocked out by Lieutenant Espinosa. Now tell us what happened just before that, and then after you gained consciousness."

"The last thing I saw was Héctor Estrada on his knees after being shot in the shoulder and bleeding, and Jesús Carillo, crying and pleading for his life. They weren't shooting at anyone, nor did I or them have any additional weapons hidden in our clothes."

A murmur arose in the hearing room at that declaration, and some members of the police force who were present shook their heads.

"What happened when you awoke?" Mr. Ayala asked.

"After receiving first aid for my head, which was bleeding, I asked those present what had happened."

"Whom did you ask?"

"Lieutenant Espinosa and Sergeant Acosta. They were in the infirmary waiting room and entered the hospital room where I lay."

"Who answered?"

"Espinosa. He said that another weapon which the subversives had somehow hidden had appeared, and that they shot first, after which a firefight had started."

"And what did you respond?"

"I said nothing. I knew it was a lie, and I would only get into hot water by saying that I didn't believe it."

"Did anything else transpire?"

"Yes, Sergeant Acosta reminded me that I was part of the team and I would be asked about the shooting. That the 'team' expected me to tell the 'truth'."

"Yet, what you have testified to so far is not what they expected, is it?"

"A murder was committed. These men were unarmed, had already surrendered, and were on their knees in handcuffs and pleading for mercy."

A deafening silence overtook the hearing room. No one even coughed.

The attorneys for the all the accused policemen and supervisors cross examined Armando López at length, but were unable to shake his testimony or cast doubts on its contents. They were only successful in having Armando López reaffirm that he did not see the actual shootings.

When the hearings ended, criminal referrals were made by the new Secretary of Justice Silverio Aponte. Charges were filed against those members of the police force complicit in the murders, and against those who tried to cover up the deeds by subsequently lying under oath in multiple investigations. Trials began for all those involved within weeks.

Sergeant Acosta, present at all the hearings, was having second thoughts about his testimony and hired a new attorney to counsel him on his next steps. He had committed perjury.

Chapter 17
Resolutions/Reconciliations

Three weeks after the El Torito debacle, Edwin received a message at his office at Casa Malatrasi that someone, a friend, had called him from the Rio Piedras Medical Center in the University complex. The message had a phone number written on it, but no name of the caller.

Edwin tried phoning the hospital several times but was unsuccessful until an orderly happened to answer. Edwin explained why he was calling, and the orderly passed the phone to a nurse, who recognized his name after Edwin identified himself and guessed the purpose of his call.

She said that a man named Ruben Collado had been hospitalized with a gunshot wound for about 10 days, and kept asking for a phone to call Edwin Ferrer, a cousin.

After a pause, Edwin asked to speak to Ruben, and the nurse said she would call him back once he was near a phone closer to his hospital bed.

A few hours later, Ruben called him.

"What happened?" Edwin started. "I haven't seen you this month at all. I thought you had left Puerto Rico for good."

"I was shot in the back by a local gang trying to collect a drug debt I owed. I survived thanks to a Good Samaritan who found me in the street and called the police immediately. If it weren't for her, I'd have bled out."

"Do the men that shot you know you survived?"

"I don't think so, since it was dark, and by the time I arrived at the University hospital, it was in the early hours of the morning."

"Then don't tell anyone your real name and why you were shot. Say you don't know."

"I already did that."

"Good. I have some bad news for you, and maybe some good news."

"What is it?" Ruben asked.

"I hired someone else to do your job, while you were absent. I couldn't wait for you to show up after two weeks had passed."

"I understand. What's the good news?"

"My brother Juan, in Sabana Grande, is desperately seeking help on the coffee farm that our father left us. He could use your help, not just as a field hand, but as an assistant running the farm. He can't do it himself. This would get you out of San Juan, and maybe they would forget about you, because if they find out you've survived, they'll come back and finish the job."

"I realize that. But I know nothing about coffee farms or agriculture."

"You will have plenty of time to learn. And Juan is a good teacher, when he wants to be."

"Can I think about it?"

"Sure, but don't take too long, because he will hire someone else."

"I won't. Thanks again for this opportunity to clean up my act."

"I'll visit you soon at the hospital, and maybe then you can give me your decision."

* * *

Fernando Díaz was an oddball in the Justice Department. Every one of his colleagues knew that he didn't belong to the party in power, so he was given the most routine and undesirable criminal cases. He had reached a dead end in his career there and was working for a supervisor who was a militant member of the ruling New Palm Party. Fernan had declined all invitations to attend office and private receptions that had a political tone to them, and therefore became ostracized by his office. He had made it clear to his coworkers that he was an independent voter now, but they didn't believe him due to his past association with the People's Party.

When the Senate investigation started, after the change in government, he volunteered to try the pending criminal cases against the police officers who were accused of murder. This included Lieutenant Espinosa, Sergeant Acosta, and the Asst. Deputy Police Superintendent, Col. Juan García, who was now accused of giving the direct orders to kill Héctor Estrada and Jesús Carrillo. Suspicions ran all the way to the Acting Secretary of State, Reynaldo Montanez, who filled in for the governor in his absence and was a right-wing fanatic.

After receiving the nod to join the prosecutor's team, he focused on fixing his personal life before the trials started. In September 1973, he went to a Bar Association Convention in Fajardo, one of many he had previously missed for past three years due to lack of interest and other commitments. But at his one, he ran into Linda Sepulveda, whom he hadn't seen for more than a year. From time to time he would ask his friend Miguel about her.

He was told that Linda had gotten engaged, no surprise to him, but after six months she had broken off the engagement when she discovered that her fiancé had another woman on the side, one who had been his high school sweetheart.

Fernan didn't know how to react to the news then or now, seeing her in person. *What should I say if the subject comes up?*

Once she was alone, he approached her, gave her a peck on the cheek as was the custom, and greeted her warmly. She didn't return the kiss, but just turned her cheek up to make it easier for her not to respond in kind.

"*Hola Linda, como estás, tanto tiempo.*"

"I'm okay, but I've had better days, and you? How is married life treating you?"

Fernan swallowed hard. Should he tell her that he had made a mistake and married the wrong woman, and that he was seriously considering a separation?

"Fine, everything is fine."

"You say that without conviction, but who am I to ask?"

"I haven't forgotten about you, and I assumed you were married."

Big mistake in saying that so soon. She was still lovely in all her ways, proud but feminine, alluring and proper, sexy, but not too obviously so in her conservative dress. He couldn't stop staring.

"Are you coming to the dance tonight?" Linda said.

"Hadn't planned on it."

"So tell me how many children you have."

"Zero."

"I see. By the way, you haven't changed much, a little gray on the sides."

"And you are as beautiful as ever, I must admit."

She smiled. "*Gracias.*"

"Would it be improper for me to ask if we could meet after the reception this afternoon for a drink, for old times' sake?"

"Yes, it would, given our history, and the fact that you are happily married, but I will accept this one time. One drink."

She was toying with him, he realized, but he deserved it. *How could he have let her go?*

Perhaps Noemí was a more refined woman, but their love life was nonexistent. Noemí detested intimate relations, and always had an excuse to avoid them. She was more interested in her figure than anything else, not having gotten over not winning the Miss Puerto Rico Miss Universe contest when she was 22. She always said she was better looking than Marisol Malaret, Puerto Rico's Miss Universe in 1970. She was not modest.

Fernan pondered his next move. Would he be honest with Linda, or let the moment pass and just live off his memories of their aborted romance?

Later that evening, after all the cocktail receptions were over and there was a three-hour break before the formal dance, he met with Linda at a small bar on a veranda overlooking the Atlantic Ocean. The Hotel El Conquistador, where the convention was being held, was relatively new and had a beautiful golf course and several different swimming pools, plus many attractions for adults and children alike. Linda and Fernan were sitting in the front part of the outdoor bar that stretched in a circular fashion, with a portion of it facing west.

After an hour or so, the sun began to set, a glowing orange ball that spread across the horizon, the type of sunset that is seen just after a storm has passed. It was an image invoked frequently in paintings by Pissarro.

Linda was the first one to speak after a lull in the conversation. The only sound in the background was of a small live trio singing romantic Spanish ballads.

"I missed you even while I was engaged, but I shouldn't be telling you this."

"So did I. I'm sorry I didn't have the courage to break off my own engagement. I was fearful of what people and my family might think of me."

"If it helps, I don't think I was ever really in love with my boyfriend. It was more like being scared of staying single, being known as a *jamona*. That's foolish, I realize now."

"It's not. Society expects that and more from young women. It always 'when are you getting married?' Or lately, like with me, 'when are you having children?' Both are improper and callous remarks. And fear not, you will never be a *jamona*. You are too special a person."

"Will you ever have kids,?" Linda asked.

"Not with Noemí. II shouldn't say never, but I don't see it happening for me."

"Would you someday want children?"

"Absolutely."

Dusk had ended. Fernan and Linda were alone in the balcony bar. More than two hours had passed and neither of them wanted that moment to end. A convention dance was just a dance, but this was a special time they might not ever savor again, so they skipped the final activity of the day.

When it was almost midnight, Fernan knew that he must make the drive back home at that late hour or spend the night somewhere else.

He did not have hotel reservations and the resort was full to capacity, due to the Bar Association meeting.

"Are you headed back to San Juan now?" Linda said.

"I guess. I'll check with the front desk to see if any cancellations have occurred and if there is a room available. What about you, are you driving back tonight?"

"My parents bought a vacation studio apartment at the lower beach level of this resort. It's technically not part of the hotel, but is accessible via the funicular that connects with the other levels of this property. They lent me the studio for the weekend."

"That's convenient. So I guess this is goodnight."

"Let me go with you to the front desk. We can say goodbye there," Linda said.

Once at the front desk, Fernan asked the clerk to see if there might have an empty room. The young desk clerk searched in vain and could not find a vacancy.

Fernan walked back over to Linda, who was sitting on a sofa in the lobby. He shook his head to convey the results.

"No luck, huh?" she said. "Were you planning to come to tomorrow's closing seminars and luncheon address?"

"I was undecided but brought an overnight bag just in case. There are some small motels nearby, so if I decided to stay, I was prepared."

"Well, no need to look for any other place. Come stay with me for the night. No funny stuff will happen. We are just friends right now, right?"

"You can't do that. What will people think?"

"There you go again. Who cares? I'm single and old enough to make my own choices. Can you believe my parents were happy with me breaking up with my fiancé? My father even said to forgive my boyfriend and give him a second chance, like my mother gave my father many times. Can you believe that, in this day and age?"

"Alright, I accept, but do you have a place for me to sleep?"

"Yes, the studio has twin beds."

They arrived at the condo studio and entered a well-appointed apartment with a spacious bedroom. The living room/bedroom was large enough to fit two queen size beds and two easy chairs with a tiny table. Behind sliding glass doors, an outdoor balcony had its own furniture.

Linda went to the bathroom to change clothes, and Fernan waited on the porch outside gazing at the full moon.

She entered the bedroom in a baby doll pajama which left little to the imagination even with a bathrobe. Fernan looked away and walked past her to change.

When Fernan reentered the room, Linda was lying on the bedspread. The robe was open. She hadn't fallen asleep.

The temptation was huge. He had not been unfaithful to Noemí, even in spite of their nonexistent intimacy. But the urge to kiss Linda was impossible to resist, so he gave in.

They had last kissed in that Condado hotel parking garage years ago. The feeling was even more intense this time. It was not a "good-night, going to sleep kiss." It was a rush of emotions which drained both of them. He took her in his arms and embraced her, almost crying.

"Linda, I still love you even after all this time. You were the biggest love of my life, and I need you."

"And I feel the same." She pulled him down next to her and kissed him passionately.

The next morning proved to be awkward. After Linda made breakfast, they ate in total silence until she said, "Do you remember what you told me last night before we made love?"

"Of course, and I meant it. This was not a one-night affair, at least not for me," Fernan replied.

"And do you realize that I can't become your mistress, Fernan? I could never do that."

"Nor would I ask you to. I had been waiting for the proper moment to fix my life, and never would have imagined it would begin this way."

"So what happens now between us?"

"I will leave Noemí and file for divorce."

"Fernan, I will hold you to that, but I won't wait forever."

"I understand. All hell will break loose, and my career will take a hit, at least in the political arena, if not in my work. I was going to leave the Justice Department soon after the trials of the El Torito cops ended. That is a service I must perform, regardless of the costs."

"Fernan, I left the government three months ago. Don't know if you had heard."

"*No lo sabía,* no."

"I joined a small all-women's law firm in Santurce, and we don't do any criminal work, only civil matters."

"I'm surprised at your decision. Won't you end up doing mostly family law?"

"Maybe. But when you leave this room today, make sure you are doing what you really want, not a spur of the moment decision, or you will come to regret it. It will get ugly for you, and if she finds out about us, I will ultimately pay the price."

"Rest assured, I know what I want, now more than ever. *Te amo.*"

Fernan packed his overnight bag, then kissed Linda, and left the room.

* * *

Edwin went to Ruben's apartment on a Saturday morning and picked up his belongings, telling his landlord that Ruben had unexpectedly left the island to go to New York on a family emergency and was not expected back for a very long time. He settled any debts that Ruben had on back rents and utilities, which were a small sum, and returned the keys to the landlord. He then drove back to his dwelling and picked up Ruben, who had spent the last few nights with him after being discharged from the hospital.

Ruben's wounds had been serious, but not life threatening, due to the prompt medical attention he had received at the University hospital. While still using a cane for balance, he was able to fend mostly alone and looked forward to other surroundings to reinvent himself. He had accepted Edwin's offer, and Juan Ferrer had welcomed him to the new life he expected to begin.

Juan Ferrer was a generous person, the older brother of Edwin who had spent his whole life on the coffee farm. His coffee beans were hailed as the best in the region, and the demand for them was high. The only thing that had held him back was his haphazard love life of a gigolo. He now had that under some but not total control.

Ruben was needed, and the training that would follow hopefully might make him successful.

There would be a transition, and Juan planned to hand over more of his responsibilities as Ruben mastered the trade. Juan knew very little of Ruben's past. Edwin had omitted some details of why Ruben had been shot, saying only that it was an attempted robbery.

"Well Ruben, here you are in the real back country of the island, where you can forget the past and really start a new life," Edwin said before he left.

"How can I ever thank you for the way you have helped me, even in light of my broken promises?"

"Just keep your head down. Remember to use your mother's maiden name on all documents like Social Security and all contact information. Get a new driver's license and keep a low profile. If you do that, your enemies won't find you."

Ruben started tearing up when he gave Edwin a final hug and said, "I'm so sorry I failed you, brother."

"Forget that, it's in the past. Move forward and make a good life for yourself here. *Eso es lo importante.*"

Edwin gave him a final embrace and walked back to his car to start the long ride home. As he drove back to San Juan, a three and a half-hour drive, he had plenty of time to think about a making new life for himself as well and planned to ask Laura to marry him. They had been dating now since she moved to Hato Rey, and he had a good relationship with Ángeles, her daughter, now a young woman. It was time.

* * *

The criminal trials against the six policemen accused of the killings at Cerro El Torito, Cayey, the night of July 4th, 1970, began on September 10th, 1974. Many obstacles had been put on the road to obtaining a conviction; individual appeals to dismiss the charges against some defendants which had failed, and also a change of testimony by Sergeant Acosta, who at the last minute sought leniency from prosecution for perjury in exchange for the true version of the events.

At the same time, federal charges were being sought by the authorities for the violation of the civil rights of the murdered men, and for perjured testimony to the FBI in its investigation of the crime. Those charges, when filed, would be part of separate criminal proceedings in the U.S. District Court of San Juan, to commence soon after the Commonwealth Courts criminal trials ended.

Fernando Díaz had been appointed co-counsel for the prosecution in one of the most important proceedings, the trial of Lieutenant Espinosa. His chief witness was going to be Sergeant Acosta, who had witnessed the entire disaster at El Torito and finally confessed to his role in the killings and to perjury. Also, Armando López was called as a witness for the prosecution.

Members of the police force called Sergeant Acosta a traitor to the police department; others with more balanced views saw him as an unfortunate man, who in his mid-40s had just ended his career.

The jury trial lasted three weeks; the decision came back in just 48 hours with a guilty verdict for murder, in the first degree, against Lieutenant Espinosa.

The flood gates opened, and trial after trial resulted in convictions of all those directly involved in the killings. Lt. Col Marrero was never convicted; three hung juries resulted in the Commonwealth finally dropping the case against him. The federal authorities passed on his trial.

Colonel García received a short jail sentence, which he never served, dying of a heart attack a few days before reporting to the correctional facility.

Armando López, in return for his cooperation with the Justice Department, and the Senate Investigation, was given immunity from prosecution from any previous unlawful activities, and no charges were filed against him. He resigned from the police force a short time later.

* * *

Carlos and María were sitting in front of the TV.

"María Antonia, who do you think was behind the executions at Cerro El Torito?" Carlos asked. "How high up do you think the order came from?"

"I believe the governor had nothing to do with it. He's a good and decent man. Maybe it was someone on his staff. But who?"

"I agree. I don't like his politics, but this is something he wouldn't have been a part of," Carlos replied.

It seems that no one assumed that an honorable politician would have ever authorized such an operation. Sadly, it was never determined who gave the order from outside the police department to end the lives of Héctor Estrada and Jesús Carrillo. No link to the office of the governor was ever proven.

Chapter 18
Epilogue

Gabriela Díaz hadn't been feeling well for some time. Her headaches grew in their intensity, and she had trouble walking by herself due to her imbalance. Doctors told her that she had high blood pressure and heart failure, which could lead to a stroke if not treated properly. They prescribed medicines and a diet. She had reached her late seventies without other major health problems, except that this one was now taking its toll.

One morning just before breakfast, she collapsed on the floor of her kitchen and couldn't get up. She lay there for hours until the housekeeper arrived and called for an ambulance when she saw Gabriela lying in front of an open refrigerator door.

Fernan and Teresa rushed to the hospital once they were notified and waited in the emergency room to hear news from her physician. Doctor Georgina Rosado, a young cardiologist, came to see them and informed that the situation was dire.

"Your mother's heart is very weak, and I can't predict a favorable outcome to her present condition. I believe it's best that she should remain here to see if she improves...or not." The doctor looked at both of them and was not optimistic in her tone or choice of words.

Both Teresa and Fernan embraced each other, thinking how it would impact Gabriela if they had told her about their own plans.

* * *

Fernan had separated from Noemí; she made a horrible scene when he left, promising that he would pay dearly for his betrayal. She suspected another woman might be involved, but she did not know exactly whom it might be.

Teresa and Julio had been making plans to move to the mainland, specifically New York, when his company closed its Puerto Rico operations and offered him a transfer to their Manhattan offices, with better pay and a promotion. He couldn't say no.

No doubt the news would have hastened the end of her life. They both felt that keeping the news from Gabriela was best then and essential now.

"Fernan," Teresa said, "I know about your separation and possible divorce, and while I have my own thoughts about that, it's your life to live, but please don't tell *Mami*."

"I won't, but you have your own news that will affect her as well."

"Yes, I know, but I will not say anything for the time being."

"What if she dies? Have you thought about that?"

"Not yet. All I remember is her wish that if she were to pass, she wanted her ashes to be buried in Barcelona, in the family plot."

"We will honor those wishes," Fernan said.

Three days later, Gabriela died. All her loved ones were present at her bedside in the hospital. She had never made it back home. A proud Catalan and fierce lover of her mother country Spain, she had found a place in her heart, for her adopted country, and always referred to the island as *my beloved Borinquen, mi Borinquen querida.* She loved the people, the culture, the hospitality, and general warmth of the population, even towards outsiders. Most of all she loved its music, which could be heard everywhere and anywhere, all the time. The only thing she despised was its politics, from all sides, which—for her—ruined the island, like it had ruined Spain.

Fernan resigned from the Justice Department and returned to his former law firm, which welcomed him back.

The quality of politics on the island had deteriorated to such a level that he had become an independent voter with dreams of joining a truly reform minded political movement that would put people first, not last, if such an animal existed. He no longer was part of the People's Party, since it had vanished with no one picking up its flag to enter the political arena.

He had a goal of becoming a senator, but with his Spanish/Castilian accent, he assumed that would brand him as a foreigner in any political forum, so he waited.

Noemí and Fernan were divorced at the beginning of 1977, nearly three years and a half years after he had had his tryst with Linda Sepulveda. He had been in constant touch with her and they dated after his separation, but did not live together until his divorce was final, something Linda had insisted on. A year after his divorce, Fernan married Linda at a small church in Isla Verde, the First Union Church, since Linda was a member of that congregation.

The wedding party was small, with only Teresa and Julio, Carlos and María Antonia, Ana Roche, Miguel Sepulveda, the bride's cousin, and her parents.

* * *

Armando López did odd jobs as a security guard at different companies for a year after the Cerro El Torito trials ended, until one day while visiting his uncle in Humacao on a Sunday morning, as he was walking up to the front door of the dwelling, a car sped past and a passenger in the car lowered a rear window and pointed a gun at him. As Armando turned around, hearing the sounds of a speeding vehicle, two shots rang out and hit him square in the chest.

He fell to the ground and lay there in a pool of blood, where he died. The vehicle raced away and no one was able to identify it for the police. Armando had gained many enemies with his honesty and paid the ultimate price.

* * *

Edwin Ferrer dated Laura Ríos for three years before finally proposing marriage. They were married at the Immaculate Church in Santurce. He had purchased a modest home in University Gardens, Rio Piedras, an urbanization not too distant from her place of work at the Teacher's Hospital. He hoped she would like it. The house was relatively modern, and certainly not luxurious, but well equipped.

Once she entered the home to see it for the first time, she was amazed at how different it was from her home in Sabana Grande, and from her relatives' home in Baldrich, Hato Rey.

"This home looks like no one has ever lived in it. When was it built?" Laura asked.

"I believe in 1960 or so. But only one family has lived in it, and after the older members of the family passed, the adult children moved away."

The one story three-bedroom house was painted in light gray with dark blue edges. The balcony was spacious, with gardenias surrounding it. A small Royal palm stood in the middle of the lawn. The house had no neighbors in front, since a freshwater canal running from the University Experimental Station bordered the property, as did the Calle Sorbonna.

"I love it, but can you afford it?" Laura exclaimed.

"No, I can't, but we will manage."

"Are you crazy?"

"I'm kidding, of course I can afford it."

She hugged him and kissed him like never before. They had been intimate before this, but were careful about where and when. Edwin loved Laura like he had never loved anyone else. Even with Emily, his first wife, it had been a different kind of love.

Laura's daughter, Ángeles, was now in her early 20s and she loved Edwin and came to consider him to be her real father.

Two nights after they had moved into their new home in University Gardens, a fire broke out at Casa Malatrasi, in the old city. The firefighters were unable to reach the eatery in time to save the structure, and the restaurant was a complete loss. The cause it was determined to be a gas leak in the kitchen.

Edwin notified Carlos Roche soon after and asked him what to do. Carlos asked to meet with him the next day to discuss the matter.

Carlos was waiting for Edwin on the front veranda of his home. He usually spent his free time watching his investments. Now he had lost one. Fortunately, the Casa Malatrasi restaurant had been insured, and in a stroke of luck due to the distance between the eatery and the *pension*, the fire had not affected the hotel. Edwin arrived at the Roche house.

"*Hola* Don Carlos, how are you?"

"I've had better days, Edwin."

"Do they know how the fire started?"

"Yes, it was the gas line to the old oven in the kitchen which ruptured."

"Are we covered for the loss, and will we rebuild?"

"Yes and no. I don't want to reopen another *fonda*."

"So what happens now?" Edwin's hands were shaking. He had just bought a new house, and now his principal place of employment was destroyed.

"I want to open a supermarket, a medium size one, but dedicated mostly to importing foods and wine from Spain."

"I've never run a *colmado*, especially a big one."

"No worries. You will become the head manager of the hotel. I have another person for the *mercado*."

Edwin was surprised at Carlos' answer. A huge weight had been lifted.

"I'm ready," he said to Carlos.

"*Bien. Para Adelante*, like my political party always said. By the way, I never told you, it was your father Gregorio who asked my father Antonio to find a place for you someday in our businesses."

* * *

After a long courtship, extended due to Héctor's unexpected demise, Ana decided to accept Francisco Rovira's offer in marriage. A University professor now with tenure, he was the opposite of Héctor, an introvert who spoke only when spoken to. It was difficult to imagine him as a teacher, let alone a college professor.

He was of medium height with dark tanned skin and fluffy brown hair. His laughter was unique whenever he let himself go. He hated politics and steered away from discussing the subject when presented. A perfect antidote for Ana, now in her mid-forties.

Francisco adored Carmencita, a young woman who had plans of her own and who accepted him as a good replacement as a father figure. Both Ana and Francisco decided on a simple wedding, no church, no lavish reception like Teresa's had been. They sought out a Justice of the Peace and said their vows. Close friends and family celebrated the union at Carlos' Condado home with a buffet dinner consisting of Puerto Rican and Spanish dishes brought in by a local restaurant.

* * *

The political climate in Puerto Rico had changed considerably from when Carlos and María Antonia were deeply involved with their respective political organizations.

The government had changed power several times since 1972, and subsequent corruption scandals in both major parties had turned the populace into skeptical voters who believed that those parties were mirror images of each other, and that the only major difference between the two, apart from the status issue, was the color of their flags. That was it. Many agreed with this assessment, including Fernan and Linda.

In that environment, Fernan sought voters like himself to form a new political entity which would place people first, and eliminate poverty, fight crime, government corruption, and build a better future for all concerned. It was the least this beautiful island deserved and which it had been denied. These goals had been the basis for the formation of the Popular Democrats in the 1940s, but these ideals had been lost or tossed aside.

Fernan asked himself if those values could ever be revived and put in place beyond the obstacles of local political infighting. He was no longer the idealistic young man who had adopted the island as his real home, but at age 55 he might still be able to do something. He realized it would take an enormous sacrifice on his behalf.

He consulted Carlos, who lately had been in ill health. When he arrived at the Magdalena house, he was escorted to the main bedroom by a nurse where Carlos lay weakened by the affliction known as Parkinson's Disease.

"Don Carlos, it has been a while since we have spoken."

"Yes it has, Fernan."

After inquiring about his health, Fernan went on to describe the sorry state of Puerto Rican politics and paused before describing his dreams for the future.

"Muñoz Marín must be turning over in his grave, from the way things have gone downhill since he died, and even way before that," Carlos said.

Fernan said, "I believe that the situation is not hopeless. I need to believe that to stay mentally healthy."

"I do too," Carlos affirmed, rising up in bed and placing a pillow as a cushion to sit up. "You sound like a young Muñoz."

"I know your history well, Don Carlos, so I have come for advice on how to channel my energies."

"Wish I could help you more than just verbal advice, which might be out of tune with present day politics."

"Anything you say will be deeply appreciated."

"Because of local politics and bias, you might be considered an outsider if you run for office. It's unfair, but that's a reality. You were born in Barcelona and speak with an accent, which will hurt your chances. So I recommend that you do become active, start a new political movement, but don't run for any office. There are plenty of good people out there that you can rely on who are fed up with the current state of affairs. Build a good platform for reform, and pick your people with care. Pick carefully the official name of the party and its slogan. Help remove the curse of petty politics from this land. It is almost as Gabriela had predicted."

The conversation lasted for five hours, Carlos was getting tired, so Fernan decided to end the chat and give his host time to rest. Little did he know that it would be the last time he would see Carlos alive.

Carlos died two months later at age 86, and a huge turnout came to his funeral. He was buried in the Old San Juan Cemetery near the old Fort Brooke Army Post, on a hill overlooking the Atlantic Ocean. It was where his mother, Paula Soler, and adoptive father, Antonio Roche, both lay. Politicians from all the political parties attended his funeral.

María Antonia Roche Oller moved from El Condado in Santurce, to the small town of Cidra, living in a mountain home facing the south coast. Lorenzo Oller, her uncle, had left her this dwelling in his will when he died. She taught Puerto Rican history, long a goal of hers, at the campus of the UPR Regional College in Cayey, until her final days.

Fernando Díaz became one of the founding organizers of a new political party, the Borinquen Renovation Party (PRB), which adopted a blue and gold colored striped flag. Linda Sepulveda and he had children of their own, as did Teresa and Julio del Valle, who settled permanently in Queens, New York. On a trip to visit his sister, at the New York airport, Fernan saw a travel poster with a photograph of a beautiful beach and palm trees which stated, "Puerto Rico, as close to

Paradise as man will ever see." He lowered this head as if in prayer, saying to himself, "*I do hope so.*"

Carmencita, daughter of Ana Roche and Héctor Estrada, entered politics after graduating with a Master's degree in Political Science from Boston University. She joined her cousin, Fernan, in his new adventure.

Sources

1. *Memorias Luis Muñoz Marín 1940-1952*, 2003, Fundación Luis Muñoz Marín

2. *War Against Puerto Ricans*, Spanish Edition, 2015, Nelson Denis, Nation Books

3. *Puerto Rico, A Political and Cultural History*, Arturo Morales Carrion and others, 1983, W.W. Norton and Company, Inc.

4. *Puerto Rico, Cinco Siglos de Historia*, 2nda Edición, Francisco Scarano, 2000, McGraw Hill Companies, Inc.

5. *Puerto Rico en el Siglo Americano desde 1898*, Cesar Ayala, Rafael Bernabe, 2011, Libros El Navegante, Inc.

6. Center for Puerto Rican studies, CUNY, Hunter College, Archives of weekly news and magazine articles, re: Puerto Rican community in New York City.

7. *The Puerto Ricans*, 2008, Wagonheim, Olga Jimenez, Luis Martínez Fernandez

8. PBS Documentary, *Latino Americans*, Episode 4, October 2020

9. *Puerto Rican Citizens*, Lorrin Thomas, 2010, University of Chicago Press

10. *Requiem on Cerro Maravilla*, Manuel Suarez, 1987, Waterfront Press

11. *Puertorriquenos en la Guerra Civil Española*, Luis A. Ferrao, 2009, Editorial de la Universidad de Puerto Rico

12. *The Battle for Spain*, Revised Edition, Anthony Beevor, 2006, Penguin Group

13. *The Spanish Civil War*, Hugh Thomas, 1977, Revised Edition, Harper and Row Publishers, Inc.

14. *Boricuas in Gotham*, Gabriel Viera and others, 2004, Weiner Publishers

15. *Puerto Ricans in America, 1948-1973*, Ronald Larson, Lerner Publications

Author's Notes and Acknowledgments

My previous novel, *Barcelona Borinquen*, a multifamily, multigenerational saga, which covered the period of 1872 until roughly 1940, in Puerto Rico left many of my readers wondering and asking what happened next in the history of those families and the island.

It took me 5 1/2 years to write that story, and my editor at the time suggested that a trilogy would be a better format for handling the time span of 70-plus years, rather than one volume, especially if I had plans for another book. But I chose to write just this sequel, to bring the narrative closer to events in Puerto Rico that occurred in the period of 30 years from 1940 to around 1973. Friends, family, and readers mentioned that they were waiting for a sequel.

I started work on this historical fiction book in the fall of 2020. My research is described on the sources page of this book. I'm eternally grateful for the hospitality and kindness of the Anibal Arocho, Library Manager, and his Assistant, Sophie, both at the Center for Puerto Rican Studies, Hunter College, CUNY.

I especially appreciate all those that encouraged me to continue writing, especially my beta readers, who once again showed up for the task of making this book better. They are Rafy Cortes, beta reader for my four novels; Nancy Haines, author of *We Answered with Love*; Carol Lach, author of *Magnolias Don't Bloom in September*; Jorge Velez, attorney and historian; and Antonio Monroig, attorney and a lifelong friend who also provided valuable background research for portions of this book. I can't thank all of them enough for their time and help with this endeavor.

My spouse, Ana Luz, read the book out loud with me, a technique which is highly recommended by many authors and editors. It helps point out what the reader might understand from the meaning of a particular passage, and it works. She has been of invaluable and essential help in all of my novels.

I also must thank my editor, David Pasquantonio, and the cover artist, Robert Thibeault. Both are friends whom I met at the Writers' Loft in Sherborn, Massachusetts, and who both helped make this book possible.

About the Author

John David Ferrer is a retired attorney and author. Educated at the University of Puerto Rico, where he obtained both his B.A. and J.D. degrees, he studied later at Boston University Law School and graduated with an L.L.M. in Financial and Banking Law. Subsequently the law school invited him to teach in the Juris Doctor program, and in the L.L.M. program as an Adjunct Professor.

His novels all describe the Puerto Rican experience at varying times during the 19th- 20th Century. The novels are *SJU/JFK* (2013), *Barcelona Borinquen* (2017), and *The Shape of Courage* (2020). This is his fourth work of historical fiction.

John David lives in the Greater Boston metro area with his family and returns to the island frequently.

.